RNWMP: BRIDE FOR KENDALL

MAIL ORDER MOUNTIES

KIRSTEN OSBOURNE

Kirsten Osbourne

Visit my website at www.kirstenandmorganna.com

INTRODUCTION

JoAnn Becker, a wealthy socialite from Ottawa, has devoted her life to music and teaching others. She is content with her unmarried status, still living at home with her parents. That is until one of her closest friends moves west to marry the Mountie of her dreams. Once her friend is gone, she feels a bit lost and confused. When Miss Hazel approaches her with a plan to send her out West to marry a Mountie as well, she agrees, not sure at all what to expect.

Kendall expects a wife just like his friend married—someone who will cook, clean, and dote on him. When JoAnn arrives, he finds that she's nothing like he expects, but everything he needs. The two of them make beautiful music together, but he's not certain it's enough to sustain a relationship. Will JoAnn agree to stay in the West and marry Kendall? Or will she give in to her insecurities and flee back home to her privileged life in Ottawa?

*M*iss Hazel Hughes hoped she wasn't sinning. She was going to church with the intention of finding just the right brides for the four Mounties who served with her son out West. Finding a woman for the youngest of the men would be relatively easy, as she already had someone in mind for him—it was the other three she needed to focus on.

As she thought about it, she realized she couldn't possibly be sinning. God wanted the men to be happy, after all. They were serving Canada, and surely God wanted the Canadian Mounties to be happy. If Canada wasn't His favorite country, why was it the most beautiful place on earth?

As soon as Miss Hazel stepped into the church, her eyes locked onto her first victim—err, bridal candidate, JoAnn Becker.

She made a beeline for the young lady, determined to convince her that going to British Columbia to marry a man she'd never met was the best idea she'd ever had.

JoAnn saw Miss Hazel rushing toward her, and she briefly considered hiding behind her friend, Lisa. It would be of no use, however, because everyone knew that once Miss Hazel had made up her mind to do something, there was no stopping her. Instead, she put on her bravest face and smiled as the woman bore down on her.

"Good morning, Miss Hazel. Have you heard anything from Theodore or Jess? We're not happy with you for taking her away from us, you know!" She glared at the older woman, determined that Miss Hazel know how JoAnn felt about her taking a third of their trio away from them to marry her son out West.

"I know, dear, I know. I want to talk to you about that, actually. Do you have a moment?" Miss Hazel asked.

JoAnn looked at the watch pinned to the bodice of her dress. It was the watch she'd been given by her parents when she'd started teaching four years before. She loved being a teacher—most of the time. "I think we have a few minutes before the service starts. What can I help you with?"

Miss Hazel seemed to debate something for a moment as her gaze shifted to Lisa, who was standing behind her. Finally, she said, "I want you to marry a Mountie as well. One of the men that's stationed with Teddy is a musician, and he needs a wife. You're the one I want to send out to him."

JoAnn frowned. She was no longer teaching a regular class, because her music lessons had really taken over. She taught piano, violin, and guitar. She preferred the violin, but so many mothers wanted her to teach piano. "Why me?"

Miss Hazel shrugged. "More of a feeling than anything else. I believe that Kendall is the right man for you—but more importantly, that you're the right woman to marry Kendall. Think about it. I'm going to start some homemaking classes for the four women who I will send out to the Mounties there. I'd like for you to be one of those students."

"But...when would you start classes?" JoAnn's mind was spinning. She wanted to marry, but more importantly, she loved the idea of living close to Jess again. She missed her friend more than she could express.

"A week from Monday. I'd like the five of us to be headed West on the first of September."

"That's soon. I—I'll have to think about it!" JoAnn looked over her shoulder at Lisa, who would be the last of their trio left if she went to British Columbia. "How do you feel?"

Lisa looked sad, but she shrugged. "If you would be happy there, you should go. I'll be fine. Just remember that you and Jess have to write at least once per week."

JoAnn patted her friend's hand. "We will." And in that moment, her mind was made up. She was going to marry a Mountie. Never in her life had she made a decision so quickly or confidently. It felt right.

JUST OVER A WEEK LATER, JoAnn took all of her belongings to Miss Hazel's house and waited in the parlor for the other three girls. She sure hoped they were women she'd like, because she couldn't imagine living as closely as they would need to live if the women couldn't be bosom buddies of hers.

The first girl hurried in looking ready to take on the world. JoAnn knew her from church, but it was a casual acquaintance. They'd never spent any real time together. Evelyn sat beside her, and JoAnn smiled. "I've seen you around church. I'm JoAnn."

"I'm Evelyn. I'm going out West to marry a Mountie!"

JoAnn couldn't help but smile. "I am too. My Mountie is musical, and that's all I really know about him. I hope he's a good man."

Evelyn waved her concerns away. "He's a Mountie. Of

course he's a good man. Mounties can fight off bears with one hand tied behind their backs. Of course, no man would have to do that for me. I'd do it myself."

"I don't know a lot about fighting off bears, to be totally honest with you. I'm more of a scholar than a fighter."

"Oh. Well, I'll defend us both then."

JoAnn shrugged. "If you can do it, I'll let you. If not, I'll throw a book at the bear!"

Evelyn laughed. "I think I'm going to like you, JoAnn. Why didn't we ever get to know each other before?"

"Because I'm too shy to talk to strangers, probably. I've been friends with Jess and Lisa since we were small, and we always stuck together."

The door opened and another girl JoAnn knew from church stepped in. Well, fell in was a bit more accurate. Rose was known for being a bit less than graceful. "Rose, who are you going to marry?" JoAnn asked. She knew a bit about each of the men because Jess had written to her about all of them.

Miss Hazel walked into the room then. "Where's our last girl? She's late?" She stuck her head out into the hallway as if that would make the mystery girl suddenly appear, but then she shook her head. "No matter. We're going to get to work anyway. The reason I brought you all here is because I want to make sure you know how to cook and clean properly before you go off to be a Mountie's wife in the West. You won't have a housekeeper out there." At that Miss Hazel pinned JoAnn with her eyes.

It was well known in Ottawa that her parents were the most well-off in town. They were odd in that they always expected their children to work for a living, though. Her two brothers were currently working their way up through their parents' furniture factory, which meant they were learning to make the furniture themselves. Both of them knew that they would end up running the company together some day, but their father needed them to know every level of the business...from the bottom up.

JoAnn tossed her long hair back over her shoulder with a hand. "I'm perfectly ready to work and work hard."

Miss Hazel nodded, acknowledging her. "Well, then. Let's get going. I'll show you to your rooms. This will probably be your last opportunity to have your own bedroom your entire lives, so I gave you each a different one. Follow me."

Evelyn frowned. "Aren't we waiting for one more?"

"Yes, we are, but that one more needs to learn that life waits for no woman. She'll be here soon, or she will lose out on this opportunity." Miss Hazel led the way up the stairs, her voluminous skirts rustling about her legs. She still wore the full skirts that were in fashion ten years ago, which JoAnn found odd. Everyone knew she had enough money for whatever wardrobe she wanted, so maybe she just liked their comfort.

JoAnn stepped into the bedroom that she was to have for the next two weeks, and she walked over to the bed, sitting on the edge of it. "This will do nicely. Will it be a problem if I practice my violin late?"

Miss Hazel shook her head. "As long as you don't get too rowdy with it, I have a feeling it will help us all to sleep." She started to close the door, but stopped short. "Be downstairs in twenty minutes, ready to work. I'll teach you how to bake fresh bread today."

JoAnn smiled, setting her things down and placing her violin on the dresser—in a place of honor. She loved her instrument. More than she loved most of the people she knew, if the truth were told. Her instrument never let her down, not like humans did. She sighed, glad the door was closed for a minute to leave her to her maudlin thoughts.

She changed her clothes, putting on an apron that covered her linen dress. Her mother wanted her to wear silk at all times, but why would someone wear silk if they were about to play in flour? Bread was made with flour, wasn't it? Truthfully, she wasn't terribly concerned about learning to cook. If she had trouble, Jess would help her. She couldn't wait to see her friend! She'd decided not to write Jess that she was coming. She'd rather surprise her.

HURRYING DOWNSTAIRS A SHORT WHILE LATER, she saw that the other girl had arrived. She was a stranger to JoAnn, who studied her closely. She had red, flowing hair, and she wore a blue dress with puffed sleeves. She wasn't wearing an apron, but Miss Hazel handed her one. JoAnn couldn't help but wonder why the girl had been so late.

Miss Hazel demonstrated making bread, and taught the girls how to knead it. She promised to send them with exact recipes of all the different things she'd teach them to cook, and at that point, JoAnn quit listening. She was a perfectly competent reader, after all. She could follow simple directions.

While the bread was rising, Miss Hazel taught them to make a simple stew, and then they all helped to clean the kitchen. JoAnn didn't particularly enjoy touching the raw meat. It was disgusting to her, and she knew her mother had never touched raw meat. No, that was something for the cook to do, not the lady of the house.

JoAnn cringed at the thought. Soon, she would be not only the lady of the house, but the cook and the maid as well. There was so much for her to learn. Why couldn't she just skip over this time and move to British Columbia to marry her Kendall? Already she thought of him possessively.

When she finally fell into bed that night, it was from utter exhaustion. She'd thought she'd have time to play for a bit before bed, but the day had been filled with baking, cooking, cleaning, eating, manners, and finally conversational ideas. JoAnn had some of the things—like manners and conversation—down better than the others, but she was sorely lacking in cooking and cleaning. Evelyn had offered to help her get better, and she could tell the other girl was going to be a good friend to her.

As she drifted off to sleep, she pictured a man in a Mountie uniform, strumming a guitar while she stood with her violin tucked under her chin in perfect playing position. They would wow all the people in the West with their skills. How could they not?

She yawned, a smile on her face as she slept. Soon she would be in British Columbia with her new husband, ready to start their lives together.

Miss Hazel woke JoAnn up the following morning with a knock on her door. She slipped into the room and sat on the edge of JoAnn's bed. "I know this is a lot for you to learn all at once."

JoAnn struggled to wake up. She was never at her best first thing in the morning. "It is," she said as she sat up, her back against the headboard and the covers tucked under her arms. "I can do it, though. I just have to put my mind to it."

"I think you can do it, but yesterday you didn't seem to care to put you mind to it. You seemed very distracted. Do you want to tell me what that was all about?"

JoAnn shrugged. "I'll try harder today. Everything you taught me yesterday...well, I just kept thinking that it didn't matter if I learned now, because Jess would happily teach me again when I got out West. And then we'd have more time that we'd be able to spend together."

Miss Hazel shook her head. "I can't send you out there

unless you know how to bake bread and make a simple meal. I know you want to spend a lot of time with Jess when you get there, and you'll be able to, but you have to be able to stand on your own two feet first. I want to know that when Jess is big with my first grandbaby that there will be a friend who can help her out."

"I'll do better. I promise." JoAnn felt ashamed of herself. Sure, Jess could help her, and Jess would be happy to do it, because they were friends. But she shouldn't have to.

When she got downstairs half an hour later, it was with a much better attitude. She'd learn anything Miss Hazel was willing to teach her, and it appeared that this morning, she was going to learn to fry bacon and make pancakes.

As the other girls watched, JoAnn followed the recipe carefully, only needing to be prodded a few times. The first pancake was a mess, because she didn't flip it quite right, but after Miss Hazel showed her once, JoAnn made the rest perfectly.

She served breakfast to her friends, along with a hot cup of coffee for each of them. When they didn't make faces, she was proud of herself. JoAnn's eyes met Miss Hazel's. "Thank you for helping me."

Miss Hazel nodded, her face filled with humor. "I'm glad you were willing to learn. It's amazing what a person can do when they set their mind to it."

After breakfast, JoAnn did the dishes with Evelyn. "You did a good job with the pancakes this morning. I was pretty impressed. I've been making pancakes for years, and yours were better than mine. I think it was the vanilla. Who'd have thought to put vanilla in pancakes?"

JoAnn shrugged. "I thought they turned out pretty well. Do you know that was the first meal I've ever made?"

"Seriously? Who cooked at home? Your mom didn't make you help her in the kitchen?"

JoAnn laughed. "I'd be surprised if my mother knew how to find the kitchen. We always had cooks and maids. No one cared if I knew how to cook or clean or do anything. I taught school for a couple of years, but only because I wasn't ready to look for a husband, and my mother gave me the choice of actively looking for a husband or getting a job. So I taught."

"I've heard you play the piano at church. You're really good. Did you have a lot of time to practice? I guess you did if you had maids and a cook."

"I probably spent as much time practicing different instruments as you spent cooking and cleaning. It was my favorite thing, so it's what I did."

Evelyn studied her for a moment. "I've always wanted to learn to play an instrument. Or sing. Maybe you'd have time to teach me after we get out West."

JoAnn shrugged. "Maybe. I have no idea what life will be like once we get there."

"Isn't your friend Jess the one who married Miss Hazel's Teddy? Doesn't she tell you about what it's like?"

JoAnn laughed softly. "Jess is so in love with Theodore—and has been since she was a little girl—that she hasn't mentioned anything other than how much she loves being married in her letters. She doesn't talk about her day-to-day life at all."

"Do you find that odd?" Evelyn asked.

"Not at all. If you knew Jess, you'd understand. She's been in a little cloud where only she and Theodore were important for a whole lot of years. I'm glad she's finally married to him, because she'll start seeing his faults. I hope she will, at least. No one can be half as perfect as she has always thought Theodore was."

Evelyn smiled. "I think it would be nice to be married to a man I thought was perfect. I hope the Mountie I marry lives up to the expectations I have in my head for a man.

Although, I'm really not sure how he could. When I think of a Mountie, I think of a giant of a man who can do anything."

JoAnn smiled. "And I picture my Mountie as a man with a guitar on his lap, singing to me while he plays."

"Do you know if that's true?"

"Yes, my Mountie does play the guitar and sing. Jess says he's wonderful, but she thinks frogs make beautiful music. The girl can't tell the difference between a instrument played in tune or out of tune. I think that's one of the things I love most about her."

"I bet you're really excited to get to see her."

"I am." JoAnn shook her head. "I don't think the two of us have spent this much time apart since we met the first day of school. I don't know what Lisa will do without us."

"Lisa? Is she the brunette girl you and Jess are always around? Is there something wrong with her arm?"

"Yes. She has cerebral palsy. Her arm works well some-days and not others. She walks with a limp but considers herself fortunate to not be in a wheelchair."

Evelyn frowned. "I guess that's why she doesn't get to go out to marry a Mountie like we do."

JoAnn shook her head. "I don't think that's it at all. I think she could be a better wife than I could. Miss Hazel is just trying to match the personalities up."

"I guess." Evelyn finished drying the dishes without another word. Her mind was obviously lost on something, and JoAnn wasn't sure if it was her friend, Lisa, or on her future.

2

$\mathcal{F}$inally, the long train ride was over, and they arrived in Squirrel Ridge Junction, an odd name for a town if you asked JoAnn. She was with the other three brides who would be marrying Mounties and the indomitable Miss Hazel.

JoAnn was exhausted. Miss Hazel had provided all their tickets, and they were in the main car, instead of in the sleeping car, which was the only way JoAnn had ever traveled. The conditions in the main car were deplorable to her way of thinking, but she hadn't dared complain. Miss Hazel had told her that she couldn't get her own ticket and travel in the Pullman car as she'd wanted, because that would be separating herself from her friends, which was unacceptable.

Each of them had brought a trunk, which was in the baggage car, and each of them had a small bag for their essentials. JoAnn had almost cried when she was told she had to put her beautiful wedding dress into a small bag, allowing it to become wrinkled. They would want to marry immediately and not take the time to get their trunks situated, and find what they needed in them, before the wedding. Hopefully Jess would be able to help her with her dress before the ceremony. How else could she send her wedding picture home and show her parents how beautiful she'd looked?

When she stepped off the train, JoAnn was staggered by the difference. She'd always lived in Ottawa. This was definitely the wild west. Why, there were so few buildings, she *almost* got right back on the train.

But no—if Jess could live in this godforsaken place, so could she. She was desperate to see her friend.

Gripping her bag in one hand and her violin case in the other, she stepped onto the platform. The first person she saw brought tears to her eyes. "Jess!"

Jess stopped for a moment in front of JoAnn, her eyes wide. Then Jess was crying too, and the two friends sobbed into each other's shoulders. "Why didn't you tell me you were coming?" Jess finally asked, swiping her hand across her face to rid herself of the tears.

"I thought it would be a nice surprise. I'm here to marry Kendall."

Jess tilted her head to one side, seeming to consider the match for a moment, before nodding. "I think you two will suit nicely. *Please* tell me you've learned to cook!"

JoAnn shrugged. "I can make pancakes, bread, and a couple of other things. I have lots of recipes written down."

"I'll help if you need me!"

"I was sure hoping you'd say that." JoAnn looked behind her at the other women who had come with her. "I think you know my friends here. Well, at least two of them. I don't know if you know Tilly. Tilly used to work as a chef, but she wanted a change, so she's here to marry Nolan. She can cook even better than *you* can!"

A man stepped up onto the platform, shaking his head. "I don't think that could possibly be true." His arm went around

Jess's waist and he pulled her close. "My wife is the best cook in all of Canada."

"Hi, Theodore. You're looking well. I think married life agrees with you." JoAnn wasn't surprised that he'd inserted his opinion into their conversation. "And Tilly's pies are the best in all of Canada! Sorry to disappoint you, Jess."

Miss Hazel was the last off the train, having gotten into a discussion with the porter about helping her with her bag. As soon as she saw Jess and Theodore, she flew at them, hugging them both at the same time. "I missed you both! Am I going to be a grandmother yet?"

Jess blushed and shook her head. "Not yet, Miss Hazel. I promise, you'll be the third to know."

"Where are the other men? Didn't they know we were coming today?" Miss Hazel asked, a frown on her face.

Theodore nodded. "Of course, they knew. Joel is in the office. The other men are on overnight assignment. They'll be here in the morning. I'm to show the women their new homes, and they can get settled this evening before the men get back."

"But that's not what I asked for. The men were supposed to be here to meet the train!"

Theodore frowned. "Mom, there's an outlaw on the loose, and they had to chase him. I'm only here because Joel decided two of us should stay in town in case the outlaw came back."

"But...what if they're not back tomorrow?" JoAnn asked. "I couldn't live out here in the wilderness all alone."

Jess shook her head at her friend. "You'll be fine. There will be lots of nights that the men are out on assignment, and we'll be here by ourselves. You're always welcome to come over to see me, or I might visit you. With five women here, we'll be able to support each other in hard times."

JoAnn nodded. "So no weddings today?"

"No idea. The pastor's in town, so if Joel wants to marry, he can. Who is Joel marrying, by the way?"

"Evelyn." JoAnn nodded toward the girl they'd both known casually for years. "She's really sweet, but she seems to think she's coming out here to *be* a Mountie, not marry one. I worry about her." JoAnn kept her voice down so Evelyn wouldn't hear her.

Jess covered her mouth with her hand. "I have a feeling Joel isn't going to like that much."

"Tell me about Kendall. You said he's musical?"

"Very musical. He sings and plays guitar. He keeps us all entertained."

JoAnn smiled. "I hope he won't mind some violin accompaniment. I brought some new sheet music as well. I can't wait to play with him."

Jess grinned. "I think Miss Hazel definitely found the right man for you. Do you want to come and help me make supper? I have a feeling everyone will come to my place to eat tonight."

"I'm happy to come over. But can you show me where *my* place is first? I could use a nice hot bath!" JoAnn was ready to sink in a hot tub. Her muscles ached from the long days on the train. Some of the girls had gone right to sleep, but she and Rose had both been unaccustomed to the traveling conditions, and she knew the other girl was just as tired as she was.

Jess grinned, as if she knew a secret. "Let's head over to Kendall's place now. I know you're not married yet, but he's given you permission to start on...I mean to move into his home."

JoAnn looked at Jess skeptically for a moment, but didn't say anything. She followed her friend toward a group of small cabins set off a bit from town. Some poor men must live there, unable to provide decent livings for their families. She couldn't help wondering what they did to make so little money.

When Jess stopped in front of one of the cabins, JoAnn gasped. "You can't mean…"

Jess laughed. "I *do* mean. You don't think Mounties live in mansions like you had back home, do you?"

"I—I guess I never thought on the kind of house they'd live in. They protect our country, so I would expect they'd be paid well and have good homes." JoAnn closed her eyes for a moment and gathered herself. She was marrying a musical man who loved his country enough to put his life on the line every day. Surely that meant something.

When she pushed the door open, the first thing she saw was his guitar leaning up against the far wall. Her eyes latched onto it, and she walked across the room to touch it gently. "It's a beautiful guitar." She picked it up and plucked the strings, tuning them automatically. She quickly played a song that had been popular back in Ottawa, smiling to herself. "I can't wait to meet him." Her words were soft and dreamy.

Jess smiled, touching her friend's arm. "The bathtub is out back."

"Wait…I have to carry the tub in?" JoAnn closed her eyes. She didn't know why it hadn't occurred to her that she'd be heating up the water for her own bath. Somehow, she'd imagined the servants doing that. She took a deep breath. "I guess I'm going to see to my bath. May I come by when I'm finished?"

Jess nodded. "Do you need some help? The coal caddy is next to the stove. You have lit a coal fire before, right?"

JoAnn bit her lip and shook her head. "No. But I'm sure I can figure it out." She looked down at her silk traveling dress.

She'd wanted to look good when she met Kendall, and the dress was ruined from the days of travel. She rolled up her sleeves and knelt on the floor in front of the stove, carefully sticking coal into it. "Am I doing it right?"

"Let me show you this first time. You don't need to get coal dust on your pretty pink dress." Jess knelt down and efficiently started a fire. "Now you need to heat up pots of water and add them to the bath. Add some cold too!"

JoAnn knew then she'd made a mistake. As soon as she met Kendall, she was going to explain to him why she couldn't possibly be a Mountie's wife and live in these rustic conditions. She was used to having a lady's maid, as well as all the comforts of living in a big city. Surely, he'd understand.

KENDALL LAY ON THE GROUND, hoping that it didn't rain. They'd been in a hurry when they'd left town—chasing the man who'd robbed the mercantile at gunpoint—and they hadn't bothered to bring a tent. In British Columbia, that was never a good thing. When it was too late to follow the trail, they'd stopped for the night, and Nolan had insisted on taking the first watch. Kendall suspected he was going to sneak some of the food out of their saddles bags, but it didn't matter. They always brought three times as much as they thought they'd need for him.

He stared up at the sky, unable to sleep as he thought about the new bride waiting for him back in Squirrel Ridge Junction. He didn't know her name yet, but he knew something without a doubt in his mind—he would give her the best life he possibly could. He imagined her to be a soft-spoken woman who could cook as well as Jess. His uniform would always be neat, because she'd keep his buttons sewn on nicely, and his clothes laundered. And she'd love to listen to him sing.

He sighed happily. His wife was going to be the envy of the other men, and he was proud of her already. Whatever her name was. She'd be Mrs. Kendall Jameson. Her looks didn't matter to him too much, because she would be perfect for him. Miss Hazel had already proven herself as a match-maker, and he trusted her implicitly.

⸻

As soon as she was finished eating breakfast at Jess's house, JoAnn headed back to the hovel that Kendall called his home. His house wasn't neatly decorated or nearly as clean as Jess and Theodore's house was. She knew it was her job to start cleaning it, but if she wasn't going to stay, was it fair of them to ask her to work hard?

She shook her head. Of course it was fair. She was about to tell a man who had been looking forward to married life that she was going back home to Ottawa because she didn't want to live in squalor. She needed to do everything she could to improve his living conditions before he returned.

She put on the apron that Miss Hazel had insisted she sew before leaving Ottawa, and she rolled her sleeves up. Cleaning this place would take months...maybe even years. It might be better if God struck it with lightning so she could start over. She hadn't noticed the filth when she first arrived, because she'd been mesmerized by his beautiful guitar. Now that she did notice it, she was more than a little disgusted.

The thing she'd learned best from Miss Hazel was how to clean. She swept and scrubbed the floors and washed the laundry, hanging his sheets on the line. She wasn't going to bother with the dirty clothes on the floor at first, but she took pity on him and cleaned those as well.

While she was hanging the clean clothes on the line, she sang a tune, her voice lifting and falling with the notes. The other women stepped outside and listened, smiles on their faces. Jess came over and gave her a hand, helping her hang each item that she'd washed.

When JoAnn had finished, she smiled, happy to be done with the chore. She hated nothing as much as doing laundry, except maybe baking bread. That was a chore she hoped to never have to do again.

Jess followed her into the house, automatically helping her scrub down the walls. While they worked, JoAnn sang another song. She could get through any kind of work as long as she had her music.

Jess and JoAnn were standing side by side, kneading bread when the door opened. JoAnn didn't notice at first, because she was still singing, her voice filling the house as it had the church many Sunday mornings. She was too shy to actually talk to people, but singing had always been a pleasure for her, and she didn't care who listened.

Kendall stood and stared at the beautiful woman inexpertly kneading the bread, and he sighed contentedly, leaning against the wall of his home. Her voice was like that of an angel. Immediately he thought about singing with her and playing his guitar to accompany her.

He didn't know the song, so when he opened his mouth to sing with her, he sang a harmony accompaniment that consisted of just notes and no actual words.

JoAnn heard the male voice and looked up, her eyes wide. For once in her life, Jess had been right. Kendall could *sing*. She stared at the man in front of her, dropping the dough onto the table and walking across the small living area toward him.

Kendall stood up straight, gazing into his future wife's eyes, knowing that he'd met his soul mate just by her voice. She was exactly what he needed. It didn't matter if she could cook or clean. She could be the very person who had robbed the mercantile for all he cared. Her voice—her *perfect* voice—it was all he needed. It would feed his soul in a way food never could.

When she finished her song, JoAnn smiled tentatively at the man in front of her. "I liked that."

He smiled, taking her hand in his. "I did too." His thumb rubbed across her palm, and he felt as if he was seeing a woman for the first time in his life. This must be how Adam felt when God created Eve from his rib. Perfection was before him, and he didn't know what to say. "I'm Kendall," he said unnecessarily.

"I'm JoAnn." She blushed prettily, feeling tingles rush from her hand where he touched it up through her body. "I stayed in your house last night. I hope that's all right." She felt stupid. Like some foreign being had stolen her ability to communicate.

"I'm glad you're here. I've been waiting a lifetime for you." He knew the words were silly, and the other men would laugh if they heard him, but it was true. He'd lain in bed as a boy and imagined a woman who could sing like she did. He'd never once imagined her half as beautiful as she really was, though.

JoAnn wanted to tell him that she was going right back to Ottawa, and she couldn't be expected to live in such primitive conditions, but all she could do was smile at him. This man wanted to marry her.

"Do you want to go see the preacher?" he asked softly. He wanted to tie her to him before she could change her mind. Being the wife of a Mountie wouldn't be easy, but he knew she was the wife for him. How could she not be? She was perfect.

JoAnn nodded, forgetting all about home and the maids waiting for her there. How could she leave this man? "I have a wedding dress."

He smiled. "I think you're the most beautiful woman I've ever seen wearing just what you have on."

JoAnn looked down at the pink cotton day dress she was wearing, and she couldn't think of a single reason she would need to change into the dress she'd had made for her wedding. She could wear it for something else. Anything else. "Thank you."

He was still holding her hand, so he led her out of his house, and toward the church. He knew the pastor was waiting there to marry them, because he'd seen him as they'd ridden into town.

When they reached the church, he called out to Pastor Wilson. "I'm here to marry JoAnn." He looked at her, embarrassed for a moment that he didn't know her last name. "I need to know your full name," he whispered.

"Becker. JoAnn Becker."

"I'm here to marry JoAnn Becker. She came from Ottawa to marry me, and she has a voice like a nightingale."

Pastor Wilson smiled, nodding once. "I see you brought your witnesses."

JoAnn turned to see Jess and Miss Hazel at the back of the church. She didn't smile. She felt like she was compelled to do everything. Each action was perfectly orchestrated and foreordained.

"Dearly beloved. We are gathered here today…"

JoAnn had no idea how much time passed, but she must have done the right thing and repeated after the pastor. When he said, "I now pronounce you man and wife. You may kiss the bride," JoAnn remembered she was going back to

Ottawa. But she was married. But she was going back to Ottawa.

Kendall turned to her, taking her into his arms and brushing his lips across hers for the very first time. She felt the kiss all the way down into her toes, and she knew she had to stay. She'd learn to cook and clean if that's what it took to be married to this wonderful man.

3

*J*oAnn couldn't stop looking at Kendall as they walked to back to his cabin. She had no idea where Jess and Miss Hazel had disappeared to, and she didn't care. Her mind was on her new husband and nothing else.

When they got into the cabin, he stopped inside the door, smiling at her. "Do you want to finish baking the bread?"

JoAnn was startled. She had forgotten putting food on the table was her job in her confusion. There was something about the man that made her brain turn into mush, and she wasn't quite certain what to do about it.

He walked over to his guitar and carefully strummed it, adjusting one of the tuning keys slightly and nodding when he had it just right. He played and sang—his accent suddenly a strong Scottish she hadn't noticed before. The song was one JoAnn didn't know, but she listened as she put the bread into the oven and carefully followed a recipe to make the chicken and dumplings Miss Hazel had made sure all of them could cook.

When he finished singing, she turned to him. "That was beautiful. I don't know the song."

"It's called 'Beauty.' My dad played it for my mother a lot when I was small. I was born in Toronto, but my parents were Scottish immigrants. Dad worked for a factory, but his true love was music. He taught me that love as well."

JoAnn smiled, happy to talk about music. "Neither of my parents like music, but my mother had in her head that a gently-reared young lady should be able to play the piano. So while my brothers were taught to work, I was sitting at my piano practicing, my music teacher at my side. I started to take lessons when I was three. By the time I was five, I had the love of music filling me so strongly, I couldn't imagine not playing. I moved onto guitar and then to violin. Now I play all three instruments, and I sing, of course. I taught music lessons back home."

"I haven't had any formal training. There wasn't enough money for that. But I have a good ear, and if I've heard a song once, I can usually play it perfectly. It takes me a couple of times to learn all the words, but I love it. I thought for a short while about becoming a professional musician, but my love for Canada was stronger than my love of music. I can be a Mountie and play music, but I couldn't be a professional musician and be a Mountie as well. I think I made the right choice."

JoAnn smiled. "It sounds like it to me. I brought lots and lots of sheet music that we can play together, if you'd like to learn something new."

Kendall frowned. "I'm sure we'll learn lots of new songs together."

As soon as JoAnn had the pot of chicken and dumplings cooking on the stove, she picked up her violin. "I'm guessing there isn't a piano in town? I couldn't bring my own, of course."

"No piano in town. But you brought your violin."

"My guitar as well. I like to play all three, but the violin is my real love."

"Do you know this?" he asked, starting to strum an old polka.

JoAnn's face lit up, and she joined the music, playing the violin as a fiddle. She'd always enjoyed fiddling instead of playing the orchestra music her mother had preferred, but she'd had to do it when no one could hear her.

When they finished the first song, she looked up to see Miss Hazel, Jess, and Theodore all standing there watching them. Jess went to the stove to stir the dumplings, and Miss Hazel set the table. "You two just keep right on playing. We'll get supper on the table."

JoAnn grinned over at Kendall, thrilled that the two of them were able to play together so effortlessly. She'd tried to play with other musicians, but they'd always needed hours of practice. Falling in with what her new husband played was so easy it shocked her. "I could get out some of my sheet music," she offered shyly.

Kendall shook his head. "We'll learn new stuff later. Let's just play for our friends."

JoAnn couldn't argue with his logic. He started on an old folk song, and she followed automatically, knowing the song well. She sang the words, and he joined her, his deep baritone voice contrasting her alto. If she'd been given the chance to choose a voice that would sound best with hers, it would have been his. She was certain she could have picked his voice out of thousands.

At the end of the next song, Jess called them to eat. "We'll go now. I was worried you'd let supper burn because you were too caught up in your music."

Kendall grinned at JoAnn. "Have you ever done that?"

JoAnn shook her head. "I have never in my life let supper

burn while I played music." It was honest as far as it went. She hadn't fixed enough suppers for that to have been a possibility.

Jess raised an eyebrow at her, obviously understanding her thought process. JoAnn waved goodbye to her friend as she left, taking her mother-in-law and her husband with her.

JoAnn walked to the table and sat down, looking around for their drinks. She realized there were none, so she got up to fetch water for both of them. "I hope you like water with your meals."

"Sure. Especially if you cook as well as Jess does." Kendall picked up his spoon.

She shook her head automatically. "I'm afraid not." She filled two glasses with the water pump and put them on the table before sitting down opposite him again. "Jess was always the best cook around. I never could figure out why she chose to work in banking when she could be a chef."

He took a bite of the chicken and dumplings. "Would you mind getting the salt and pepper?"

She frowned. At home, there would be a maid to fetch them, but here, it was up to her. She hurried over to the counter and pulled down the spices out of a cabinet. "I'm sorry if I didn't add enough." She thought for a moment, wondering if she'd added any. No matter, he was adding some now, right?

"What was your life like back in Ottawa?" he asked. "I know you obviously had time for your music."

"I've been a school teacher for the past few years, and I would teach music after school. Other than that, I guess my life was pretty normal."

"Did you live with your parents?"

"Yes, and my brothers. They both work for my father's furniture factory. They'll run it together one day, but for now, they're starting at the bottom and working their way up. Father doesn't think that his children should be given anything on a silver platter, and we should always work for what we have. That's why I was teaching as well. I've saved every dime I've ever made."

Kendall eyed her for a moment. Their worlds couldn't be more different. "Sounds like your upbringing was very different than mine. My parents were immigrants, and Dad *worked* in a factory. He certainly didn't own one. There were six children in my family. Do you have sisters?"

She shook her head. "No, there were just Thomas, Andrew, and me. I sometimes think Mother would have liked to have another daughter, but she was rather sickly."

"My mum took in washing to help make ends meet."

"My mother had tea parties three afternoons a week. The most work she ever did was directing the servants." JoAnn frowned. "Do you think less of me because my upbringing was privileged?"

He shook his head, taking another bite of her chicken and dumplings. He hoped she and Jess would work together to get her cooking up to scratch. As it was, he was having a hard time getting it down. "Not at all. It just means we won't have as much in common."

"We have music. Do we need more?"

Kendall considered her question. "Probably not. I guess I just thought I'd be getting someone who was good at domestic chores, and instead I've gotten a wife who is a musician and a debutante."

"If the queen ever comes to tea here in town, I will be the person who will know how to serve her. My manners are impeccable."

"I have a feeling that's never going to happen."

JoAnn shrugged. "But if it does..." She suddenly worried that he would find her lacking. She remembered her emotions when she'd first arrived in Squirrel Ridge Junction, and how she'd wanted to get on a train and go straight back to Ottawa where she belonged. Was he finding her inferior?

"I guess I just need to wrap my mind around not getting exactly what I thought I'd get."

"Are you disappointed?" She didn't have a lot of experience with the opposite sex, but she knew that a direct question was always the best way to get the answers you needed.

Kendall thought about that for a moment before answering. "I'm married to a beautiful, talented lady. No, I'm not disappointed. Surprised is more the word that fits."

JoAnn nodded. "I'm happy you don't find me lacking." She worried about his hesitation though. Shouldn't he have answered right away that he was pleased with her? Somehow, they didn't seem to be starting their marriage off on the right foot.

After she washed and dried the dishes—with no help from him—she walked back to her fiddle and picked it up. He had been playing and singing softly the entire time she worked. "Do you want to try a new song now?" she asked softly.

He shook his head, again playing a song she knew, and she immediately joined him, wondering what he had against her new music. She had to admit that it was fun to play old favorites with him.

As they played together, the hours seemed to disappear. Before she knew it, she was yawning. She set down her violin. "I need to get some sleep if I'm going to be worth anything tomorrow. It takes all my concentration to cook. I'm not at all like Jess."

He walked close to her, touching her for the first time since the wedding ceremony. Cupping her face in his hands, he looked deeply into her eyes. "I don't want you to be like Jess. I want you to be like *you*."

She smiled, a bit sadly. "You want me to cook like Jess."

He shrugged. "Doesn't every man want a woman who cooks well?"

"I don't know. Do they? Maybe you should learn to cook and cook for us both."

He frowned. "I have to work all day."

"I'll be cleaning and doing laundry all day. Did you even notice all the work I put into your cabin while you were out?"

He nodded. "I did. I should have said something. I'm sorry I didn't."

She sighed. As they grew to know one another better, he would understand the things that she needed from him. "Where are you going to sleep tonight?"

"What do you mean? There's a bed. I'll sleep in it."

JoAnn frowned. "Then where will I sleep?"

"We're married. We'll share the bed."

"You can just get that idea right out of your head. I'm not sharing a bed with a man I met a few hours ago. Have you lost your mind?"

He frowned. "Are you planning on sleeping on the floor then?"

She shook her head emphatically, walking over to the spot where he'd dropped his bedroll when he'd come in that afternoon. She picked it up and carried it to him. "Here you go. The floor or outside."

"Do I at least get a kiss goodnight?"

"I don't see a problem with that." JoAnn was annoyed with him, but she wasn't certain why. She wanted him to compliment the horrible supper she'd made and fight for his right to sleep in the same bed with her. Why wasn't he acting like a new husband should?

He walked closer to her, leaning down and kissing her, his lips lingering on hers. "I hope you sleep well." He walked over to the spot beside the front door and rolled out his blanket, not even looking at her again.

JoAnn went into the bedroom and closed the door, changing into her nightgown. She hoped marriage wouldn't always be this awkward.

JoAnn woke to the sound of pounding on her bedroom door. She groaned and covered her head with her blanket. It was too early for her to have to be awake. The door opened, and Kendall stuck his head in. "Are you going to fix breakfast?"

She groaned and rolled over, wanting to go back to sleep. "Yes, I'm coming. Give me a minute." She knew that being married meant seeing to his needs first, and he needed breakfast. She wanted to tell him to just go to Jess's for breakfast as she knew he'd been doing since her friend married Theodore, but she also knew it was the wrong thing to do.

So she got up, quickly changed into a day dress, and hurried into the kitchen. He'd already started the fire. "I started the coffee. I thought that might help you."

She smiled over at him. "Are pancakes all right?"

"I love pancakes." He sat at the table and watched as she got the bacon out of the ice box and awkwardly cut off several slices so she could fry them. She didn't seem as comfortable in the kitchen as Jess always was, but when she put his pancakes in front of him, they tasted as good as any he'd ever tasted. "These are delicious!" He was thrilled to be able to compliment her cooking after the disaster of the night before.

JoAnn's face lit up at the compliment. "Thank you!" She sat across from him, and cut into her pancakes, taking a bite.

They *were* good. She was thrilled to know he was being honest. "What will you do today?"

"I have to go out on rounds. We're going in pairs for the whole week, because we weren't able to catch the man who robbed the mercantile on Wednesday. He did it at gunpoint, so he's got to be considered dangerous."

"Could you get hurt?" She barely knew him, yet she worried about him being injured. She wasn't sure if she would miss him as a singing partner or as a life partner. Either way, she didn't want anything to happen to him.

He shrugged. "A Mountie could always get hurt. I could be thrown from my horse. I could get shot. Any number of things could happen. I'm careful though."

She frowned at him. "You'd better be. I'm not ready to be a widow just yet."

He smiled, recognizing her words as a compliment. "I'll do my best."

As soon as he was done, he stood up and put on his hat. He was already dressed in his Mountie uniform. She stood and walked to him, raising her lips for his kiss. Before yesterday, she'd never kissed anyone but family, and now here she was acting as if kissing her husband was normal. "Stay safe."

She crossed her arms over her chest and watched him go, saying a quick prayer for his safety.

Her day was again filled with chores. She went to talk to Jess about what she'd done wrong with the chicken and dumplings. "I want to cook a delicious meal for supper, but I obviously don't have the talent. I tried to follow the recipe exactly, and I could barely choke it down. I don't know how Kendall resisted spitting it out."

Jess shook her head. "Just be glad you're not married to Nolan. That man is always hungry. I swear he's got a hollow leg. There's no other explanation for where the food goes."

JoAnn frowned at her friend. "So you'll teach me to make something?"

Jess shrugged. "I'm making a pork roast tonight. Why don't you make the same thing, and we can fix them together? You can watch me, and then I'll watch you. There'll be a better chance of you getting it right if you see me demonstrate, and then I watch you to be sure no errors are made."

"All right. I should bring in the clothes from the line first, though, right?"

Jess frowned. "Did you leave them out there overnight?"

"Yes. Shouldn't I?"

"Let's go get them." Jess led the way, explaining as they went. "It rains so much here. If it rains, you'll have to redo everything."

"But the rain would just wash the clothes, wouldn't it?" JoAnn didn't understand what the big deal was.

"The rain would make mud and puddles, and the clothes would be splashed. You need to be more careful than that with the laundry."

JoAnn frowned. "I'm not sure I'm ever going to get this stuff right."

"You will. I'll help you. And remember, you can sing like nothing he's ever heard."

4

*W*hen they got out to the clothesline, Jess frowned. "There's that silly moose again."

JoAnn looked at Jess and then over at the moose, who was standing with her clean sheets on his back. Or was it a her? What did she know about the gender differences of mooses? Meese? Moosi? "Jess, what's the plural of moose?"

"Moose." Jess shook her head. "Bull moose can be dangerous, but I've seen this one around. He's mischievous, but he doesn't seem at all threatening."

JoAnn looked at the huge creature. "Could I pet him?"

"I wouldn't recommend it. He could kill you with a kick."

"But he looks so friendly…"

"Just stay back. We'll get the laundry in later."

"But what if it rains, you said…"

"JoAnn, I love you more than just about anyone. You've been one of my closest friends for a lot of years. Don't make me end that friendship with your early demise." Jess walked in the back door of JoAnn's new home. "Do you need some help with the windows?"

JoAnn looked at her windows and frowned. "I guess they do need to be washed, don't they?"

"Of course, they do. And it's your job to do it." Jess grinned at her friend. "The maids aren't going to pop out of the bushes and start washing your windows, you know!"

"I know. If they were going to pop up and do anything, they'd cook for me. Do you have any idea how much I hate cooking?"

"No one likes every aspect of their job," Jess said, getting to work. "We really should make curtains for your windows. You'd have a little more privacy that way, and they'd look so pretty."

JoAnn wrinkled her nose. "Of course, we should." She shook her head. "How are the other girls? Have you heard?"

Jess nodded, her face seeming amused. "Two are married, one is not. I don't know that anyone is happily married just yet. I don't know why Miss Hazel thought that everyone would look at each other and fall madly in love. As far as I can tell, you and Kendall came the closest to that, and I don't think you're as much in love with him as you are with his music."

JoAnn shrugged. "He does have a lovely voice. I am definitely not in love with him, though. I barely know the man."

"I can't imagine being married to a stranger. It would seem so odd sharing a bed…"

"Oh, I made Kendall sleep on the floor! I told him I haven't known him long enough for those types of shenanigans."

Jess burst out laughing. "I'm sure that went over well."

JoAnn bit her lip. "I probably shouldn't have said anything about that to you. Please don't tell anyone!"

"Oh, you know I will guard your secrets with my life. Remember when we were little girls and I'd write you a note when I was supposed to be doing my arithmetic? And I spelled secret S-E-E-K-R-I-T? I think that's when I told you that I was in love with Theodore, and I'd grow up and marry him."

JoAnn grinned at the recollection. "And you did grow up and marry him."

"Thanks to my meddling mother-in-law." Jess finished scrubbing the window she was working on and went on to the next. "I think we should go over to the mercantile and choose some fabric for curtains. When I made curtains, it made our little cabin so much homier."

JoAnn sighed. "A grand piano would make this place so much nicer, don't you think?"

Jess laughed. "Where would you put it? You'd have to take out the table."

"Then we could eat every meal at your house and I'd never have to cook again. I *like* this plan."

"We'll go to the mercantile after lunch."

"I suppose we will."

<hr />

WHEN KENDALL GOT HOME LATE that afternoon, he opened the door, saying a little prayer that his wife had asked for help with supper. Her pancakes had been superb, but he'd rather eat sand than her chicken and dumplings.

She was standing at the stove, carefully stirring something that he hoped was gravy. Something smelled wonderful. "What are you cooking? It smells delicious!"

JoAnn looked at him with a smile. "I'm attempting gravy by myself for the first time ever, so you might want to try just a little to see if it's edible. I did my best, but that may not count for much."

"What else did you make?" He was skeptical about her gravy, but something did smell very good.

"Pork roast, potatoes, carrots, and fresh bread."

"Sounds good." Kendall removed his Mountie jacket and hat, hanging them on hooks by the door. "How much longer until it's ready?"

"Just a minute or two. As soon as the gravy thickens properly, I'll set the table. *If* the gravy thickens properly." JoAnn frowned down at the pan she was mixing the gravy in. "Maybe I didn't add enough flour."

Kendall left her to sort the gravy out and picked up his guitar, strumming it automatically and playing an old love song from Scotland. His father had often played it for his mother, and his mother had always swooned. He sure wished JoAnn would swoon over his playing. It would make his night so much better. She didn't seem to be a swooner, though.

JoAnn felt the music wash over her, listening to the words Kendall sang as he strummed his guitar. His voice had gone all Scottish again, which surprised her. Usually there was no accent to his words, because Canadians didn't have accents, but when he sang specific songs, it was as if he was transported to the highlands of his ancestors.

She finally got the gravy thick enough—she hoped—so she pulled the roast out of the oven and put it on a plate, put the carrots and potatoes into a bowl together, and served it all. She set the table and put glasses of water on for each of them, congratulating herself that she'd remembered drinks before she sat down. Putting salt and pepper in the middle of the table, she sat down, proud of how everything looked.

Kendall finished the song and set the guitar down, meandering over to the table. "Everything looks good!" He took a piece of the bread and buttered it. After taking a bite, he smiled at her. "Bread is wonderful. Did Jess help?"

She shook her head. "Not with the bread."

"Well, I'm impressed then. You're not as bad a cook as I

thought you were." As soon as he realized what he'd said, he frowned. "I didn't mean it like that."

JoAnn sighed. "Yes, you did. I promise I'm not completely useless. I just never learned to cook. My mother never expected me to come to the West and marry a Mountie."

He served himself some meat and potatoes, unsure of the gravy. He decided to wait until she'd tried it before he attempted it. Taking a bite of the meat, he nodded. "Very good!" As he mashed his potatoes with his fork, he asked, "What did your parents think about you coming here?"

She shrugged. "My mother thought I'd lost my mind, but my father said that it's good I want to be out on my own. He believes that we make our own dreams, and it was time for me to set out to figure out what my dreams were."

"You never wanted to be a professional musician?"

"I wanted it for a while, but my mother was mortified. She thinks that women of good breeding don't belong on any kind of stage. So I gave up that dream to be a teacher. I taught for a few years, but I was about to only do music lessons this year. I gave up my teaching post. I prefer to teach music anyway."

"Which do you prefer to teach? Piano, violin, or guitar?"

"My favorite thing to teach is music theory. I like to show a student how to transpose into a new key and how to make sense of music."

He looked at her for a moment with a confused look. "I don't know much about any of that. I play by ear." He was almost embarrassed to admit it after what she'd just said.

"You don't read music? Really? Usually, I can tell, but you're very good! Would you like me to teach you?"

"I'm not sure. I'll think on it."

She frowned, her fork halfway to her mouth. "You love music. You can't read music. But you don't know if you want to learn? What would stop you?"

"It would just seem weird learning from my wife."

"If I needed to learn something from you, would that be strange?"

If he'd looked up to see the look on her face then, he'd have been warned, but he was too busy toying with his foot. "Well, no, because you're my wife. You're supposed to learn things from me."

She stared at him for a moment, her mouth agape. "Did you really just say that? So you can teach me things, but I can't teach you things because I'm a *woman?* What is the difference?"

"Well, a woman is meant to learn from man. He's meant to guide her in all things."

She blinked for a moment. "I see."

When he looked at her then, her face was slightly red. "Are you feeling all right? Your face is…darker than it was."

"I'm working hard to control my anger. Do you really think that because you have a penis, you can teach me things…but I can't teach you anything, because I don't have one?"

"I didn't say that!" She was twisting his words all up, and he wasn't having it.

"What *did* you say then?"

"I said that the man teaches the woman. It's the natural order of things."

It took every ounce of discipline JoAnn had not to dump the potatoes over his head. She envisioned herself doing it though, and it made things easier for her. She looked at him and saw a big chunk of potato mixed in with one of the curls in his dark hair, and she felt slightly better.

"I'm not sure if we should be married," she finally said. "We don't have the same outlook on things."

"No, maybe not, but we can both compromise."

"I'm not sure if I have the ability to compromise quite that much." She frowned at his plate. "You didn't even try the gravy."

"Neither did you!"

"I made it for you, not for me."

Kendall frowned. "If I try the gravy, will you forgive me for saying stupid things?"

"Do you admit they were stupid?"

"I'm not sure. Do I have to admit they're stupid if I eat the gravy?"

JoAnn stood up from the table, and took the gravy to the sink. She pumped some water into the bowl and carried it to the slop bucket, where she poured it out. He didn't deserve her nasty gravy. He deserved nothing from her.

He stared at her, wondering what he'd said wrong. "I guess eating the gravy isn't going to get me out of trouble, then."

She frowned at him. "You have a very bad attitude, Kendall. I'm not sure I even want to be around you anymore tonight."

"Why not?"

"Because you're making me crazy! Trying to get me to forgive you by eating my gravy. It's like you're comparing eating my cooking to torture!"

Kendall stared at her, confused. "That's not what I meant!"

JoAnn spun on her heel, trying to keep the tears at bay. She was angry, not sad, and she had no intention of letting him see her tears. She hated when she cried when she was angry. "What did you mean, then?"

"I—I don't know!"

JoAnn counted to ten, and then she counted backward down to one, taking deep breaths the whole while. "Why would you move your mouth without knowing what you meant to say?"

"I—" He frowned. She was right. "I'm very sorry for saying bad things about your gravy before I ever tried it. I'm sorry that I said I wasn't sure if I could learn from you. Of course, I can learn from you. I'd be happy to learn from you. Will you please teach me?" He had to make her happy after being an idiot. One of the few pieces of advice he'd gotten from his father about marriage rang in his ears.

His father had once said, "Son, it doesn't matter if you think you're wrong. It doesn't matter if you know you're right. Apologize and beg your wife's forgiveness. It's the only way to make your marriage work."

JoAnn frowned at him for a moment. "You really want me to teach you?"

He nodded eagerly. "Maybe you could teach me after church tomorrow? We could go for a walk after lunch, and you could teach me how to read music when we got back. I'd sure love to be able to write down some of the—" He stopped there, knowing he'd already said too much. The songs he'd "written" were for him and no one else.

She eyed him for a moment. "Do you write music?"

He felt trapped for a moment, but he didn't want to lie to her. He closed his eyes and nodded, wondering what she'd think of him. "A little. I have the words written down, and I know what notes I play, but I don't know what the notes look like, so I haven't written the music."

"But you'd like to write the music?"

"I guess so."

She cleared the table and poured the water she'd heated into the sink to wash the dishes. "All right. We'll start tomorrow."

Kendall stood for a moment uncertainly, watching her wash the dishes. Was she still angry with him? "Would you like me to dry the dishes for you?"

She looked over her shoulder at him, and considered

letting him do the work, knowing he was only doing it to get back into her good graces. "No, you worked all day. I'll do the dishes." Though, she'd worked all day too. He should be able to see that, shouldn't he?

He walked over and picked up his guitar, uncertain of what else to do to get on her good side. He played a popular love song, singing along with it, hoping it would mellow her mood. He'd been told many times that he sounded better than the original musician who recorded it. Thank God he had a Victrola, or he'd be completely lost with contemporary music.

As she did the dishes, she heard him start singing a familiar song. It had been the most popular song a few years back, and it was one she loved. As she listened, she sang along with him, loving that he'd chosen "In the Shade of the Old Apple Tree."

By the time the song was done, she had walked to him, wiping her hands on her apron as she went. They finished the song looking into each other's eyes, and she reached out, resting her hand on his arm.

He didn't take a moment to think before he leaned forward and brushed his lips against hers.

When he'd pulled away, she studied him for a moment. "You make me absolutely crazy—but when you kiss me, my toes curl, and I want it to go on forever."

Kendall grinned. "I'm going to take that as a compliment."

"Oh, you definitely should. Except the making me crazy part. I wish you'd stop that nonsense."

"I'll do my very best. I never want to make you crazy. I guess I'm just good at it."

She sighed. "That you are. I've known you for two days, and already you've made me crazier than anyone else in this world…except maybe my brothers. They both made trying to make me lose my mind a favorite avocation."

"I have to admit that I was the same with my sisters. It was fun." He shrugged at her. "Go finish the dishes, and I'll sing for my supper."

She leaned close to him and pressed a kiss to his cheek. "I'll play with you after the dishes."

"I was hoping you'd say that." As he watched her head back to the sink, he strummed the first few notes of another Highland love song. Hopefully by the end of the month, she'd know as many as he did. He loved sharing his culture with her in the form of music.

JoAnn had a slight smile on her face as she finished the dishes, pleased that he'd apologized in the most spectacular way he knew how...through music. He was a good man from what she could see, but he wasn't very well trained in being a husband. Her mother had told her just before she left Ottawa that a man didn't come to a woman knowing how to be a good spouse. He had to be taught by his new wife.

Thankfully, she knew herself to be a very good teacher. She'd have him whipped into shape in no time. How could she not? She had the language of teachers and the language of love. If he didn't understand one, she knew he understood the other.

---

*J*oAnn enjoyed church the following day. Miss Hazel sat between her and Jess, insisting that they shouldn't be near enough to one another to whisper through the sermon. JoAnn frowned at the older woman. "We haven't whispered through church in months!"

"Only because you haven't been *in* the same church for months!" Miss Hazel responded.

Jess smiled at JoAnn. "Don't worry. She *has* to go home sometime!"

Miss Hazel shook her head, looking over at Theodore. "Teddy, you're going to have to do your best to keep these young ladies under control when I'm gone!"

Theodore shook his head. "I'm only responsible for one of them. Talk to Kendall about the other."

Miss Hazel leaned around JoAnn to see Kendall. "You will see to your wife, I presume?"

Kendall was tongue-tied around Miss Hazel, as usual. After a moment, he managed to say, "I don't think there's any point in trying to *see to* my wife, ma'am. She has a mind of her own, and I'm mighty fond of her that way."

JoAnn looked at Kendall for a moment, absolutely beaming. It was the nicest thing anyone had ever said to her. "Do you really feel that way?"

He nodded, almost frightened. Had he given her license to be one of those women's libbers that he kept hearing about? He wanted to tell her not to take the compliment too much to heart, but he was afraid to take it back now. He didn't know if she'd hit him over the head with her violin.

"You couldn't have said anything that would have made me happier," she said with a grin. "Thank you, Kendall."

Thankfully, Pastor Wilson called the congregation to order then. "This morning we're going to start with 'What a Friend We Have in Jesus.' Please rise to your feet while we sing."

JoAnn slid her hand into Kendall's and wove her fingers through his. Neither of them needed a song book for such a common hymn, so they sang together, their voices rising and falling perfectly together. It wasn't until the last note faded away that JoAnn realized everyone else had stopped singing and were watching her and Kendall. She leaned to Kendall and whispered, "Were we too loud?"

"No, I think we were so good they forgot to sing while they listened!"

JoAnn felt funny, but she hadn't done anything wrong, so she simply sat down when the pastor asked them to. She leaned into Kendall, liking his feeling of strength against her.

After the prayer, the sermon was on marriage and working at getting along with your life mate. Very appropriate considering all of the new marriages there in Squirrel Ridge Junction.

Once the service was over, JoAnn spent a moment talking to Rose, the only girl with a similar background to hers. "How's marriage?"

Rose shrugged. "I won't speak against my husband, which means I probably shouldn't answer that question."

JoAnn bit her lip against a laugh. "I think we probably would have interesting stories were we to sit down to tea together. Don't you?"

"Has it been hard for you as well?"

"Of course it has. I married a total stranger, just as you did." JoAnn sighed. "It seemed like a good idea at the time, didn't it?"

"Would you go back to Ottawa and forget him if you could?"

JoAnn looked over to where Kendall was talking to Joel. "No, I don't think I would. I mean, I'd think about it, but Kendall and I are obviously meant to be with one another. The way our voices blend together tells me that."

"You can't think you belong together just because of how you sound. That's silly."

JoAnn shrugged. "It is how I feel. He's a good match for me. What about you? What do you think of Elijah?"

"He needs a haircut." Rose crossed her arms over her chest and looked across the church at Elijah, where he was talking to the pastor. "He makes me just a little bit angry sometimes."

"I'm sure he does. That's what husbands are meant to do, isn't it?"

Rose grinned a little. "Well, maybe."

"Where's Tilly? I'm surprised she's not here." JoAnn looked around the small congregation once more, just to be sure she hadn't missed the other girl.

"Oh, she's with Mr. MacGruder. He was shot when the mercantile was robbed, and she's cooking for him and making sure he's comfortable." Rose laughed softly. "She probably refused to let him come to church."

Kendall walked over. "Are you ready to go?" he asked softly.

JoAnn nodded. "Yes, let's go."

As they walked the short distance back to their cabin, Kendall asked, "What was your friend looking so upset about? What's her name anyway?"

"That was Rose. She's just dealing with some troubles. No big deal." JoAnn didn't feel comfortable talking about her friend's problem with her husband. What if he told Elijah what she'd said? No, it was better left between her and Rose.

Kendall looked at her strangely, but didn't ask again. "What are you fixing for lunch?"

JoAnn sighed. "I never realized what a burden my family was on the cook back home. We all expected to eat three times a day just like you do. Why do people think they need to eat three times a day? Why isn't once enough?"

He wondered if she really expected him to answer that. "Umm…"

She went straight to the ice box and pulled out leftovers from the previous night. "We're having cold sandwiches, and that's that. I won't try to make a gravy for them, because I'm sure you won't eat it anyway." She looked at him. "Any objections?"

He shook his head, realizing there was no other wise course of action. There was no way he was going to make her happy unless he just agreed with her at the moment. She wasn't going to cook anything else anyway. He walked into the bedroom and changed. She'd never seen him in anything other than his Mountie uniform, which he wore even to church, so it would be a change.

When he went back out into the main room, he was wearing casual slacks and a blue button-up shirt. "Do you want to go on a picnic?"

JoAnn nodded, grabbing a basket from the work table.

She wrapped the sandwiches in paper and then put them into the basket, adding some extra bread and a jar full of water. "I'm ready."

He looked at the basket, not saying a word. Jess would have included a dessert…but he wasn't married to Jess. And Jess had a tin ear. He'd realized that when she'd first arrived. He didn't know if he wanted to be married to a woman who couldn't sing, but that didn't matter anyway. His wife had a lovely voice. Why he still had Jess in his head as the perfect wife, he didn't know. Maybe because she cooked so well. That must be it.

"How long have you known Jess?" Kendall was thrilled to have found a safe subject that wouldn't make her angry. If they had many more fights during meals like they'd had the previous night, he was sure he'd have indigestion.

"We met our first day of school. There were three of us who were always together. Jess, Lisa, and me."

"What's Lisa like?" he asked. He hadn't heard Lisa mentioned before, but he hadn't spent any time at all alone with Jess.

"She's really sweet. Jess and I started working after we finished our schooling, but Lisa couldn't. Her arm doesn't work right, and she limps, so she does a lot of charity work. She loves animals, and she has this tiny little dog named Sophie that she talks about all the time, and she takes everywhere with her. She even took her to church one day!"

"Oh, wow. Your pastor allowed that?"

JoAnn shrugged. "It was a big church, and Sophie was in a picnic basket. Only Jess and I knew, and we giggled and giggled."

"So Miss Hazel wasn't kidding when she said Theodore and I need to keep our eyes on you two."

"I think we've outgrown that kind of thing." JoAnn didn't mention that it had happened less than six months ago. Now that she was an old married woman, it felt juvenile to have found it so funny.

"That's too bad. It's always funny to see an animal get loose in church."

JoAnn laughed. "Jess and I kept thinking it was going to happen. We'd see the lid of the basket move a little, and we'd both start laughing again. It was a good thing I wasn't singing that day, because I'd have never made it through a song. My mother took me to task that afternoon. She was not pleased with my behavior."

"Well, I think she should have been. Sounds like you were using one of the qualities God gave you in abundance."

"What's that?" she asked.

"Humor!" Kendall grinned at her as he stopped beside a bench in front of the small lake at the edge of town. "Do you want to eat here? I think this is a beautiful spot for a picnic."

She nodded, sitting down and arranging her skirts around her. She put the picnic basket beside her on the bench and opened it, handing him his sandwich. "We're going to have to share the water. I didn't think to bring two jars or glasses."

He shrugged. "We're married. I don't think it'll hurt anything if we share a drinking glass."

Once they were eating, she looked out across the lake. "There's that silly moose again. He got all tangled up in our laundry yesterday."

"He's been causing some trouble in town. I want you to stay away from him."

"But why? Jess said he just seems to get into mischief, but he isn't dangerous."

Kendall shook his head. "Don't you go thinking you're going to make a pet out of that silly moose."

"Why? I was going to name him Mickey Moose. Don't you like that name?"

He wrinkled his nose. "Mickey Moose sounds stupid. Why does he need a name? He's not a pet!"

She shrugged. "He's around so much that I think he should have one."

"If you see him without me around, I want you to go straight inside and shut the door. A moose can kill you very easily."

"Mickey would never kill me!"

Kendall didn't think that statement deserved an answer. "I want to teach you to shoot."

"Why? I'd never shoot anyone or anything. You're not suggesting I shoot Mickey, are you?"

"Stop calling him that. He's a wild animal. Wild animals do *not* need names. But yes, I would like you to know how to shoot so that you could kill him if he was threatening you. Or what if a bear came after you?"

"A bear? Are there *bears* around here?"

"You're living at the edge of the wilderness in Canada. I'd say it is the wilderness, but the town is here, so it's not really the wilderness…but yes, there are bears here. Why would you think there wouldn't be?"

She shrugged. "I guess I didn't think bears went into towns very much."

"They don't, but this is mostly in the country, not the town. There are bears. I promise. You need to be able to shoot to protect yourself. Unless you already know how to shoot?"

She laughed. "Sorry, learning to shoot bears or meese or moosi or any other wild thing was not part of my drawing room education. I'm so sorry about that."

"I guess it wouldn't have been. What's a meese or a moosi?"

"I like those words better for the plural for moose. It

doesn't really feel like it should be the same word for singular and plural, does it?"

"Yes, it does. Moose is the plural and the singular. Not meese."

She made a face. "You're a real spoilsport sometimes, Kendall."

He shook his head at her. "I'm really not. I am serious about my work and keeping my wife safe, though, so we're going to have those shooting lessons. Do you want to start after our picnic?"

"I thought I was going to teach you to read music after our picnic. What happened to that?"

"I can learn to read music after dark. You can't learn to shoot after dark. We have a little shooting range made up out in the woods. I'll show you."

"What if a bear or a moose stumble on you while you're practicing? Do you shoot him for being in his own territory while you're out there playing with your gun?" she asked. She knew she was being difficult, but she really couldn't see herself shooting any of God's creatures.

He frowned at her. "If an animal threatens me, yes I shoot it."

She swatted at a mosquito on her hand. "You're welcome to shoot the mosquitoes, but not the moosi. I like them."

He chose not to correct her word choice again. If she had to call them meese or moosi, it wouldn't hurt him any. She would be the one looking silly, not him. "Mosquitoes are a little too small to shoot."

"If I run into a bear, may I name him Bob? Bob Bear sounds really nice."

He groaned. "You want to name the moose Mickey, and a bear Bob. You like alliteration or something?"

"I love it. I think that any time two words are together, they should start with the same sound. Don't you?"

"Not particularly. I guess I can live with it though. Just promise me you won't name our first son James Joshua Jameson, though."

"Oh, of course not. He'd be Joshua James. Has a better ring to it, don't you think?"

Shaking his head, Kendall got to his feet. "Let's head back. I want to grab my other gun, and I'll show you how to shoot."

"Your other gun? Are you saying you brought a gun on a picnic with your new bride?" JoAnn frowned up at him.

He held a hand down to help her up. "I always have a gun on me. It's my duty to keep you and the citizens of British Columbia safe. I'm always on the job and prepared. It's part of being a Mountie."

"And you obviously take your job very seriously," she said. As they walked back to town, hand-in-hand, she sang a little song. "So shooting and then music? I do want you to learn to read music. We'll be able to do so much more with our music that way."

He nodded. "All right. We can do that." He still didn't feel comfortable letting her teach him anything, but he wasn't going to tell her that again. She'd made it very clear the night before that she didn't like him saying so.

JoAnn didn't like her first shooting lesson. The gun hurt her hand when it jerked back. "Just let the bears eat me. Evelyn made it really clear that she could handle a bear bare-handed anyway. Get it? Bare-handed?" She laughed at her joke while Kendall glared at her.

"Are you finished joking around? This is serious. You need to be able to protect yourself." He reloaded the gun. "Now, watch me this time. You have to use the sights to line up your shot." He glanced over and saw her still giggling at her own joke. "Will you please pay attention?"

"I'm trying. I just forget how funny I am sometimes."

Kendall demonstrated the perfect shot one more time before handing her the gun. "Now you try it."

"My hand is going to hurt so much, it's going to be hard to play my instruments. I don't know how you do it."

"I'm used to it, because I've practiced. Remember how much your fingers hurt when you first learned to play the guitar? Now they probably don't hurt at all. That's because you've practiced and gotten used to it. You need to do the same with your gun."

"I can't. I don't have a gun."

"Now you're just being difficult." Kendall sighed. "Shoot the rest of the bullets in the gun, and then you can be done for the day. We'll walk back to town and you can teach me to read music."

"You're going to love the freedom that reading music gives you." She turned to talk to him, the gun swinging around toward him.

He caught her wrist, and carefully pointed the gun down. "Don't ever point a gun at someone unless you plan to shoot them. So don't ever point your gun at your husband!"

"I have a feeling that in the years to come, you'll be the person I want to shoot more than any other. Don't you think?"

Kendall shook his head with a sigh. "You're going to be nothing but trouble to me, aren't you?"

She grinned, turning back toward the target and taking careful aim. She emptied the gun, hitting the target with two out of the five bullets. "I did it! I did it! Did you see that?"

He nodded, pleased with her enthusiasm. "You hit the outside of the target, so it would be like shooting a bear in the arm instead of in the gut, but you did it."

"So now we never have to practice again because I did it, right?"

Kendall shook his head at her. "Every weekend until I'm sure you could kill a bear before he got to you."

"How many weekends will that be?"

Probably the rest of our marriage. "I'm not sure. We'll see how you do!"

"You don't think I'll ever get good, do you?" JoAnn asked him skeptically.

He shrugged. "I don't know. You might!"

She glared at him, but gave him the empty gun and watched him carefully check to make sure there were no bullets left before putting it into his holster. "Now for music lessons!" She couldn't believe how excited she was to share her love of music with someone else who obviously loved it as much as she did. "I'm going to teach you the treble clef first. That's what you need for the guitar. But I'm going to teach you the bass clef as well, because you'll need that for singing."

"Why would I ever need music for singing? I hear it once, and I can sing it."

"Because you need to be able to see it when you look at it and hit all the right notes." She held his arm and spoke enthusiastically as they walked back toward town. "I promise, you'll love it!"

"Whatever you say."

hen JoAnn first pulled out some of the sheet music she'd brought with her, Kendall blanched at just the sight of it. He took a deep breath and took the page from her, looking at it. To him it just looked like strange lines. "My dad is the best musician I know. He spent a long time trying to learn to read music, and he couldn't ever figure it out."

JoAnn frowned. "It's really not that difficult. Did he have a teacher?"

"He did." Kendall shook his head. "I think maybe because my dad couldn't do it, I have in my head that it's too difficult for me."

"Well, it's not. You're an intelligent man."

"Are you saying my dad wasn't?" he asked, not sure if he should feel complimented or offended.

"No, of course not. Some people are better in life than they are on paper, though. One of my most intelligent students, who memorized every single lesson and could do arithmetic like nothing I've ever seen, didn't have the ability to learn to read. He would stand up and recite the reading from the night before by memory, because his mother had read it to him."

"That's strange. I never saw my father read. Mom would read him the paper every morning before he went off for the factory."

"What my student told me was the words danced on the page. I don't know if your father had the same problem. Did he have the opportunity to go to school when he was young?"

Kendall shrugged. "He never talked to me about his schooling. I know he was the youngest of ten children, and he helped with the family farm. I don't know if he helped because schooling wasn't a possibility, because they needed him on the farm, or because he just couldn't learn."

"I'm not sure, but I do know you have the ability to learn this. You read, don't you?" she asked. She was sure he did, but she asked just in case.

"Yes, I've been reading since I was a small boy. My father insisted all of his children knew how to read young. Mother would sit and work with us, and then when we went to school, we were ahead of the others."

"Then let's get started. I know you can learn this." She taught him the secrets she knew to learning the lines and spaces on the treble clef, explaining how to use FACE and 'Every good boy does fine.' By the end of the evening, he could play some tunes just using the notes in front of him.

"That was wonderful!" she praised after he'd played 'Twinkle Twinkle Little Star.' "You're a very fast learner."

"But you're having me play baby songs I already know."

"In a different key, though, so it's not the same." She put the music down for the night. "Now we should just play something we enjoy singing together."

"Maybe we should talk a little. Get to know each other better." Kendall felt like he knew her musically, but as a wife, she was still a virtual stranger.

"We could. I'm pretty boring without my music, though."

Kendall shook his head. "I have a very hard time believing that."

"You do?" JoAnn was surprised. Most people accepted her words at face value when she said she was boring, because it was true. She loved to sing and play, but all of her spare time was taken up practicing.

"What do you do for fun?"

She shrugged. "I play my violin, guitar, or piano. I sing."

"You were friends with Jess and…what was the other girl's name? Lisa? What did the three of you do together?"

JoAnn's face softened into a smile. "We spent a lot of time talking. We jump-roped some, but Lisa had trouble with lots of physical things. Sometimes we played games where we had to think. We loved to play charades together."

"See? You did things that weren't musical then. What game was your favorite?"

"You won't laugh?"

"Of course not. Why would I laugh?" Kendall wasn't sure what she was going to tell him, but he knew he'd never laugh whatever it was.

"I like to play chess. I'm really good at it."

"Really?"

She nodded. "It was my father's favorite game, and he started teaching me about the time I started my piano lessons…so when I was about three or so. I haven't lost a game in a whole lot of years." She'd gotten so good she could beat her father and both of her brothers.

"Did you bring a set with you?" he asked.

"I did. Do you play?"

"My father taught me as well. I've never beaten him."

"We'll have to play!" She ran for her trunk that had been pushed off to one side in the main room, knelt in front of it, and rummaged through her things. When she found the small travel chess board, she pulled it out and carried it to the table. "We can play chess and still talk. It's not like music."

He grinned, sitting across the table from her. "Let's play."

They played for the rest of the day, only taking a short break so JoAnn could make a quick meal of bacon and pancakes. They were fairly evenly matched. She won five games, and he won four.

"I've never played with anyone as good as you are," she told him, absolutely delighted to find someone else who could play. It had never been easy for her to play with only people who were not as good as she was. Of course she enjoyed winning, but it was a lot more fun when it was actually a challenge.

When it was time for them to go to their separate beds, she felt that their day had been a success. Not only had they each taught the other something that was very important to them, they'd found more common ground. Now if she could only learn to cook to his expectations, everything else would be—dare she say it—gravy.

WHEN JOANN WOKE up the following morning, she was feeling more positive than she had since she'd arrived in Squirrel Ridge Junction. She was up before Kendall, and she hurried as she made the only breakfast she knew how to make.

When Kendall woke, he could smell bacon, the aromas filling the small cabin. Nothing was nicer than waking up to the smell of bacon. He stood and walked over to where his new wife was standing in front of the stove. He wrapped his arms around her waist from behind, and kissed her cheek. "That bacon smells fabulous."

JoAnn removed the bacon from the frying pan and set it onto a plate. Then she turned in his arms, wrapping her arms around his neck. "I didn't even burn it this morning!"

He laughed. "That is definitely appreciated." Leaning down, he brushed his lips against hers. "What are your plans for the day? You know I'll be out all night, right?"

JoAnn frowned at him. "No. Where will you be?"

"A few of the territories are too far to visit in just one day. We take turns with our overnight trips. Tonight is mine. If you get nervous, I'm sure Miss Hazel would be happy to come and stay with you." He hated the idea of leaving her alone overnight when she couldn't really shoot yet, but he really didn't have a choice. Besides, the other Mounties were in the area, and they would be able to watch out for her.

"I don't like it, but I guess it's part of being a Mountie's wife. And I sure do like my Mountie." She stood on tiptoe and brushed her lips against his again. It was strange thinking that she could kiss this man whenever she wanted, but they were married, and that made it all okay. "I think I will ask Miss Hazel to stay with me. I'm sure Theodore and Jess are getting tired of having her be there all the time. So they'll probably enjoy a little alone time."

"It would honestly make me feel better if you weren't here alone. I like the idea of Miss Hazel staying with you. She'll make sure you don't get into trouble."

JoAnn laughed. "You've only seen the sweet, motherly side of Miss Hazel. That woman is absolutely crazy. Some of the things she got up to back in Ottawa, well... I'm not going to go into any details. Suffice it to say it would be enough to make you prematurely gray."

He grinned. "I see the mischief in her eyes. I think she

could do some pretty crazy stuff." Hugging her close for another moment, he said, "I need to go get ready for the day. No one takes me seriously unless I'm wearing my red serge jacket."

"I'll make the pancakes while you get you change." When he was almost to the bedroom door, she called, "And Kendall?"

He turned and looked at her. "Yes?"

"I really like your red serge jacket."

He went into the bedroom, smiling to himself. He was going to get sick of pancakes before too terribly long, but hopefully by then she'd have learned to cook something else.

After he'd gone for the day, JoAnn walked over to Jess's house to ask Miss Hazel if she'd spend the night at her home. Miss Hazel looked her up and down as if seeing her for the first time. "You know I'm not going to help you work, right?"

JoAnn shrugged. "That's fine. I just don't want to be alone."

"And you're going to fix a decent supper for me? I don't want any of that nasty stuff you've been feeding Kendall."

JoAnn bit her lip. "Has he complained?"

"No, but I know you can't cook. Maybe I'll spend the day teaching you to make a couple of more decent meals. The man's going to start protesting if he gets pancakes three meals a day forever." Miss Hazel walked to the mattress that was on the floor in the main room. She picked out a few things and put them into a bag. "Jess, I'm staying with JoAnn overnight. She needs to be able to make a few more meals so that poor Kendall doesn't revolt."

Jess bit her lip, obviously fighting laughter. "I think that's a great idea."

JoAnn glared at her friend. "Where's the loyalty?"

"You need to be able to cook. Have a nice time." Jess

seemed truly relieved to see JoAnn abscond with her mother-in-law.

"Let's go pick some apples," Miss Hazel suggested. "I know of a small cove of trees outside town, and I'll teach you to make apple pies, because I know you weren't paying any attention when Tilly gave her pie-baking lesson."

"I was…"

"You were not!" Miss Hazel shook her head. "Let's get a couple of bags to put apples in."

JoAnn had found a couple of burlap sacks while cleaning the house. She handed one to Miss Hazel, and the two of them left town, walking away from the lake. "I'm not sure I'm quite ready for pie yet, Miss Hazel."

"Pie is easy. I'll show you. Tilly makes them kind of fancy, and I think you need more basic instructions. And you need to make some applesauce too. I think that would make Kendall happy." Miss Hazel stopped at a small grove of apple trees.

JoAnn reached for the apples she could reach, but she knew there was no way she could fill both bags. She was more than a little shocked when she turned around to see Miss Hazel in a tree, straddling a branch. "Miss Hazel! Come down! You'll get hurt!"

"I may be older than you, but I'm not elderly yet, and I'm still feisty. I can do it." Miss Hazel carefully stood up on the branch and began picking the apples, her feet unsteady.

"I'd feel a lot better if you weren't in that tree endangering yourself." JoAnn looked at the distance to town and thought about running for Joel, but she didn't know what she'd do if Miss Hazel fell while she was gone.

"Oh, don't get your drawers in a bunch! I'll come down when I'm good and ready!"

"Uh oh! Mickey Moose is coming. I promised Kendall I'd go straight home if I saw him, because he says meese can be dangerous." JoAnn looked up at the older woman imploringly, hoping she'd get out of the tree so they could go back to her house.

"Meese? JoAnn Becker, you need to stop calling moose meese, and stop calling Monty Moose Mickey Moose. May I ask what your problem is?"

"My problem is that my name is now JoAnn Jameson, and I didn't know his real name was Monty. I like Mickey!"

"Well, I named him Monty, so you can find some little mouse to name Mickey. The moose is Monty, and that's that." Miss Hazel looked down at JoAnn. "Come and hold your bag open under me so I can drop apples into it. It looks like it might rain, and I'm not coming down until both bags are full."

"But what about Mickey—I mean Monty Moose? What if he hurts us?" JoAnn asked, eyeing the moose who was ambling their way.

"Teddy says he's perfectly safe. He'd probably eat the apple right out of your hand." Miss Hazel hit JoAnn in the head with an apple.

"Ouch! Watch where you're throwing those things." JoAnn rubbed her head for a moment, before opening her bag wide again. "Kendall won't like it if I don't listen to him and go back to the cabin with the moose on the loose." She giggled. "I like that. Moose on the loose!"

"Just hold the bag and stop rhyming, silly girl!"

When both bags were full, Miss Hazel looked down at the ground. "I'm not sure I can get down."

JoAnn's eyes widened. "How can I help?"

Miss Hazel sighed. "Go see if Joel is in the office. He'll get a ladder and help me down."

"Will you be all right for as long as it takes me to run there and get him?" JoAnn felt like she was doing something wrong by leaving the older woman trapped at the top of the tree.

Miss Hazel maneuvered herself until she was sitting on the branch once again. "I'll be fine. But do hurry."

JoAnn ran to town, and once she was there, she realized she didn't even know where the Mountie office was. She quickly saw the sign for it—it wasn't like there were a lot of businesses in town—and she rushed inside, finding Joel sitting at his desk, frowning down at some paperwork. "Miss Hazel's stuck in a tree!"

Joel frowned at her. "How'd she get into a tree to begin with?"

"She climbed. We were picking apples, and she made a horrible decision to get up there, even though I begged her to come down. She said you might bring a ladder."

He got to his feet. "I'll run home and get a ladder. Where is she?"

"There's a small grove of apple trees, just outside of town."

"I know it. You go be with her, and I'll find you."

JoAnn ran as fast as she could back to the tree, looking up at Miss Hazel. "He'll be here as soon as he gets a ladder. How are you doing?"

Miss Hazel shrugged. "I'm a pleasantly plump old woman stuck at the top of a tree. How do you think I'm doing?"

"At least you have snacks up there if it takes us a while to get you down." JoAnn wasn't sure if she should be laughing or crying. She was just thankful Theodore wasn't in town to see that she'd gotten his mother stuck up a tree.

"Well, let's pray I won't be up here long enough to need a snack."

Joel came along then with a ladder, standing beneath the tree and looking up. "Looks like you've gotten yourself into a fine predicament, Miss Hazel. Why did you decide to climb a tree today?"

"We were picking apples, and there were lots of apples we never would have been able to reach from the ground, so I decided I should climb the tree. Anyone looking at JoAnn would be able to tell she'd never figure out how to climb a tree." Miss Hazel frowned down at Joel. "Are you going to get me down or not?"

"Of course I am. As a Mountie, it's my job to help people in need. Whether I'm helping catch bank robbers or helping women who are old enough to know better out of trees they never should have climbed."

"Don't rub it in now, Mountie!" Miss Hazel sat impatiently waiting for Joel to get the ladder into place.

JoAnn stood to one side, wringing her hands together. "How can I help?"

"Stay out of the way," Joel told her, climbing the first few rungs of the ladder. "Won't you join me, Miss Hazel?" He offered her a hand to help her feel steady, and she was able to turn around and back down the ladder with him always one step beneath her.

When they reached the ground, Miss Hazel hugged Joel tightly. "Don't you ever tell Teddy I did that!"

Joel laughed. "I'm happy to have something to blackmail you with, Miss Hazel."

The older woman laughed and reached up to kiss his cheek. "You're a good boy, Joel." She turned to JoAnn. "And you weren't much help at all. Never mind. Let's head back to the cabin. It's time for me to teach you to make apple pies."

Joel's ears perked up. "Did someone say apple pie?"

Miss Hazel rounded on him, her hands on her hips. "I'll bake you your very own apple pie if you'll promise never to tell Teddy about this little incident."

Joel grinned. "You have yourself a deal, Miss Hazel. I'll expect payment while the pie is still hot."

"You'll get it!"

JoAnn shook her head, trailing along behind Miss Hazel, carrying the two bags of apples. Life had been a whole lot easier back in Ottawa. Of course, Kendall was *here*.

7

*B*y the time Kendall got home the following evening, JoAnn had three new meals she could cook, and there was an apple pie waiting on the table. Kendall walked in, looking out of sorts, and JoAnn went to him, hugging him tightly. "I missed you." She hadn't realized it was true until she said it, but she had missed all of his little habits. No one had played music for her, and without him, there hadn't been much desire to sing. It was strange how quickly she'd grown used to having a husband around.

Kendall smiled, pressing his face into her hair. It had been a rough couple of days, and he was so happy to be home. "I missed you, too. I've grown accustomed to having you here with me."

"How was your trip?" she asked, not sure what all she was even allowed to ask about what had happened. Was there a Mountie code of honor where they couldn't mention things that had occurred?

"It was long. There was a land dispute. There are two farmers about a day's ride from here who argue about six feet of land. Each of them have over fifty acres, and there's six square feet that they've been fighting over since I came here a few months ago. Theodore says it's gone on a lot longer than that." He shook his head, sitting in one of the chairs at the table and rubbing the back of his neck. "When I arrived, the two of them were standing there with rifles drawn. I've caught them that way at least three different times. They just can't seem to give in about this tiny little piece of land."

JoAnn served the stew she'd made into a bowl and put it in front of him, along with a glass of water. "Who owns it?"

"That's the thing. No one is really sure. There was a tree marking the line between their land, but that tree was chopped down for firewood years ago, and the stump burned. They've been fighting ever since."

"How old are they? Sounds like too old to be acting like children."

"Definitely." Kendall took a bite of his stew, ready to spit it back out if he needed to, but it was good. "They've got to be in their sixties. I talked to their wives, who are close friends by the way, and they both said to let them shoot each other because it'll save them a lot of grief."

JoAnn shook her head. "Sounds like a ridiculous kind of situation to me."

"It is. I'm not sure what to do, but I'll be talking to Joel about it tomorrow." He looked around the cabin, noting a few more subtle changes she'd made. "Anything exciting happen while I was gone?"

"Miss Hazel taught me to make apple pie, and I have one ready for you to try. I made it all by myself, but she watched, so I'm sure it won't poison you." She related the story of apple picking. "I wasn't sure what to do. Monty Moose was running around, and you told me to go inside if I saw him, but Miss Hazel was stuck up that tree. What should I have done?"

"Sounds like you did the right thing." He shook his head. "What did Theodore say about that whole thing?"

"That's the thing! She bribed Joel into not telling him with an apple pie, and she made it very clear to me that if I told him I would never be forgiven. So I didn't say anything."

Kendall laughed. "Sounds like Miss Hazel. I love that crazy old woman, but she does the darnedest things sometimes." He took another bite of stew. "This is really good. Did you make it yourself?"

She nodded. "I did! Miss Hazel watched, and I think it turned out pretty well." She served herself a bowl and refilled his before taking her seat opposite him. "It was strange having her here instead of you."

He smiled, reaching over and taking her hand in his. "I would have been here if I could. I'm glad we have a place where you won't be the only woman around. Some Mounties are the only white person in the whole area, because they're assigned to areas where they're surrounded by natives. You'll have it easier than most."

"What if you get reassigned?"

He shrugged. "I guess we cross that bridge when we come to it. Do you like it here?"

She nodded emphatically. "I like the other women I came out here with, but my special friendship with Jess makes it a good place for me."

"We should have the others over and play music for them. Let them dance."

"Really? Would you do that?"

He nodded. "I did it all the time before. Now that you're here, we can play together."

"I'd like that." She smiled. "Talk to the others and see what day is good. It would be nice to get to know the other Mounties, and see how the other women are with them. I have to wonder if Miss Hazel did as well with the other matches as she did with ours."

Kendall grinned, taking another bite of his stew. She thought they were a good match. It warmed him from the inside out hearing her say that.

IT WAS time for Miss Hazel to leave on Thursday, and all of the ladies were gathered at the train platform to see her off. When it was JoAnn's turn to say goodbye, she hugged the older woman tightly. "I'm going to miss you so much."

"Oh, pshaw. You're not going to miss me at all. You have Jess here, and you have a new husband who is going to demand your time. You won't have the time or inclination to miss me," Miss Hazel whispered softly to JoAnn. "Learn three new dishes a week. Soon you'll be cooking as well as all of the rest of the ladies."

"Except Rose. No one wants to cook like Rose."

Miss Hazel just winked at her, moving on to hug Jess one last time.

As they walked back from the train station, JoAnn linked her arm with Jess's. "What are you fixing for supper tonight?"

"Fried chicken. Teddy loves my chicken with mashed potatoes and gravy. Why?"

"Because I need to learn to cook something new. Poor Kendall is sick of pancakes for every meal."

"All right. I'll show you. It's easy."

JoAnn groaned. "Every time you tell me it's easy to make something, I know it's going to be hard."

Jess patted her arm. "You're exaggerating as usual."

"I'm really good at two things. Music and exaggerating. Everything else positively befuddles me." JoAnn followed Jess into her cabin, noting that the extra mattress that had been placed there for Miss Hazel was already tucked neatly away. Jess seemed to actually enjoy doing housework, though JoAnn had no idea how any woman on earth could. It was boring, and a drudgery in her eyes.

Jess looked at her friend. "Go home and get a frying pan, pot, potatoes, chicken, and flour." She went on to name several other things JoAnn would need.

"Are we feeding the whole town, or just Kendall and me?"

"Just go get the ingredients, and I'll show you how to make use of them."

JoAnn sighed, stepping outside to go do as she was told. She didn't want to cook. She wanted someone else to magically make food appear on her table like she was used to.

Three hours later, she was stirring the gravy on the stove at her house, knowing it was perfect this time because Jess had stood over her as she carefully mixed in the flour and the milk.

When Kendall came in the door, he inhaled appreciatively. "Something smells really good!"

JoAnn smiled at her husband, her heart jumping at seeing him. "Jess helped me, and I took notes. I really think we're actually going to be able to eat it."

He walked to her, stooping down to kiss her cheek. "How was your day?"

"It was good. We all went to the train station to say goodbye to Miss Hazel. She's going to be missed around here."

"She is. When she left last time, if felt like a hole was in her place in our little town. Even though she left Jess, so we had someone making wonderful meals for us and a feminine presence, it wasn't the same." He shrugged. "She's a really special lady."

JoAnn frowned. "Well, I know I'll miss her." She watched as he stripped off his Mountie jacket and hat, appreciating his shoulders. "Supper's ready. I just have to serve it."

He sat down at the table, his eyes watching her every movement. He was ready for her to be his wife in every sense of the word, but he was afraid to bring it up. "Your cooking gets better every day."

"Are you trying to flatter me, Constable Jameson? I assure you, I'm going to let you eat regardless."

"You are incorrect if you think I'd ever stoop to flattering you to try to get supper. No. I am hoping you'll consider sharing that big bed with me, though." He watched her carefully, wondering how she'd react. The subject had been left unspoken for long enough that it *had* to be brought up. They'd been married six days now, and they got along better than a lot of married couples he'd met.

JoAnn bit her lip. The idea of sharing a bed with him made her nervous, but it was his right. How long would he agree to sleep on the floor in the main room? "I suppose we could discuss that." She set the plate filled with fried chicken in the middle of the table, then went back for the mashed potatoes and gravy. After serving them each a glass of water, she sat down across from him, noting his astonished look. "What?"

"I just didn't expect you to agree so readily."

"I didn't agree. I agreed to talk about it. That's something else entirely." JoAnn put a scoop of potatoes on her plate and topped them with the creamy gravy. She'd stolen a taste while she was stirring them, and it was the best gravy she'd ever had the pleasure of eating.

Kendall filled his plate, carefully looking at everything. He knew he was being unkind by worrying that it would kill him, but her cooking *wasn't* always the best. He put a tiny bit of gravy on the mashed potatoes, and after taking a bite, he grinned. "This is fabulous!"

"Now don't you wish you'd tried my gravy the other night?" she asked.

He frowned. "Will you ever forgive me for that?"

"Sure I'll forgive you, but I have a long memory. I *won't* forget about it. Ever."

He sighed. "I should have known better. How about I make up for it by eating every bite on my plate and then getting seconds."

"Are you sure you want to make that offer before even trying the chicken or the green beans?" She bit her lip at the look of fear that passed over his face.

"Well, maybe I should try just a taste of them first."

JoAnn laughed, shaking her head. "You are not a very trusting man, are you?"

"I just don't want to get sick. If I'd eaten any more of your chicken and dumplings, I'd have been *very* ill!"

"You just don't have any respect for the work that goes into feeding you. Alas, I'll spend the rest of my life laboring away for a man who has no appreciation for me. Woe is me!" She put the back of her wrist against her forehead in a dramatic pose.

Kendall bit into the fried chicken and sighed happily. "This is really good!"

"I know." JoAnn took another bite of her mashed potatoes before cutting off a piece of bread and buttering it. "Bread's good, too."

"Your bread is always amazing." He piled more potatoes, gravy, green beans, and chicken onto his plate, then buttered himself a piece of bread.

"You're eating like it's been months since your last meal!"

He shrugged. "It seems to be feast or famine around here. I'll feast while the food is good, and then I'll be able to skip a couple of meals when they're disgus—err...not to my liking."

JoAnn shook her head at him. "I'm getting better. It's just

taking some effort. I thought because I could follow instructions, I could come out here and follow any recipes. There's more practice involved than that, unfortunately."

"I'm sure you'll be as good as Jess and Tilly in no time."

"Tilly? Have you heard about her cooking already?"

Kendall nodded. "Yeah, Nolan brags about it every day. I know you've met him, but have you ever seen him eat? I swear the man could go to a church potluck and push everyone else out of the way to eat every single bite of food himself."

"Really? He's so thin. How can he eat that much?"

"We've all wondered that. I have no idea. I swear he must have hollow legs. I've seen him eat three times what everyone else eats, have room for dessert, and still steal someone else's food. He's a mess."

JoAnn looked shocked. "Wait—he's a Mountie and he steals food? Isn't that against your moral code?"

"It should be against *everyone's* moral code, but he says that he's a growing boy, and we should all be willing to share our food with him."

She sighed. "He sounds like someone I really don't *want* to get to know."

He shrugged. "He's a great guy. Everybody loves him, and we all continually forgive him for stealing our food."

"Well, I certainly don't know why. Unless the food was like my chicken and dumplings the first night."

"Nope. We even forgive him for stealing food Jess has made."

"Sounds like he's got to be a good man, or no one would ever forgive him." She got to her feet, carrying her plate to the sink. "Are you done eating? Or would you like me to wait to start the dishes?"

"No, I'm done. I think I'm going to work a little more on learning to read music. I want to figure it out. I didn't even know what the strings were called on the guitar until you told me." Kendall stood and walked toward where his guitar was leaning against a wall, always in the same spot except when he played it.

While she worked, he picked out a couple of songs, and then he strummed a chord. "What chord is this?" he asked.

"That's a C." JoAnn had perfect pitch, and she'd always been able to hear the different sounds in the notes, naming them correctly.

"How about this?" He played another. He played all the chords regularly, but he wanted to be able to call them the right thing when he was talking to her. He was suddenly obsessed with learning all the notes and the chords and reading music properly. He wanted to be as well-versed in music as she was, now that he knew how easy it all was.

"G." She kept washing the dishes, randomly calling answers to him over her shoulder.

After a little while, he stopped playing with the notes and started playing again. He played yet another Highland love song for her. His voice rose and fell as he strummed the chords in accompaniment.

JoAnn put the last dish away before she turned and walked toward him. His music was like a siren's call to her, making it impossible for her to keep her distance. She walked over and picked up her violin, playing an accompaniment softly. She'd never heard the song before, and she didn't want to not hear the ending.

By the time the song was over, she had tears coursing down her face. "Your music is beautiful."

He smiled. "Do you play the music of your ancestors? Where is your family from?"

She shook her head. "My family has been in Canada, or the British colonies, for four generations. I don't know any of the songs of my German ancestors. I wish I did."

"Well, at least you can play polkas with the best of them," he said with a wink. At that he transitioned into a fast-paced polka that had her laughing as she fiddled right along with him.

When they were done, she put her violin down. "My mother was always against my using the violin as a fiddle. She said it was a beautiful instrument, only suitable for the orchestra. I love playing it as a fiddle though. Just know we can never do it when she's around."

"Do you think we'll see her often?"

JoAnn shook her head, feeling a bit homesick. "No. They're too far, and Mother doesn't like to travel."

"That's too bad. I'd like to get to know them."

She looked at him, thinking about all the reasons he was perfectly suited to her, but she knew her parents would never like him. No, she wouldn't take him home often. There was no need to put either of them through that.

8

*S*unday was another shooting lesson. JoAnn hated holding the gun, but she knew that Kendall would have a hard time feeling safe without her learning. As she stood with the gun held tightly in both hands, she carefully squeezed the trigger, missing the target and hitting a branch in the tree a good five feet higher than her goal.

"I hate this!" she said. "I don't even like holding this thing. It feels dangerous!"

"It *is* dangerous, which is why you're learning to use it properly." He sighed, walking toward her, but making sure to stay out of the line of fire. She was still waving the gun around like it was a toy. "I know you hate it, but if you can't use it, how am I going to be able to leave you while I go out overnight? How can I trust you to stay out of Mickey Moose's way?"

"Monty Moose."

He stared at her in confusion. "You called it Mickey before."

"I didn't know Miss Hazel had already named it Monty

Moose." She shrugged. "I have to listen to her. I think she would wallop me otherwise."

He shook his head. "Fine, Monty Moose it is. Why would she wallop you?"

"I'm not really sure. But I think she would. She wasn't happy when I kept referring to meese either. She said I had to learn to say moose."

He had no idea how they'd gone down this conversational path, but they needed to be steered back to the shooting lessons. "You need to be more careful with your aim."

"Do I have to learn to shoot? Can't Evelyn learn and protect us all? She was sure she could defend us before we even came out here."

"I don't care if Evelyn can shoot. I care if *you* can shoot, because I want you safe."

She sighed. "But I don't like shooting. Maybe I can learn to use a sword. Or I can learn to play a really high note on a flute, and it would shatter the eardrums of any creature trying to hurt me! Would that be okay instead?"

Kendall looked at her like she'd lost her mind, which she had to admit to herself, she probably had. She didn't want to shoot, so she was talking about absolutely ridiculous things that weren't even within the realm of possibility to get out of it.

"No. You will learn to shoot." He pointed back at the small target he'd nailed to a tree. "I want you hitting the center of the target nine times out of ten."

"I see. You want to be married to Annie Oakley."

"I want to be married to JoAnn Jameson, but I want her to learn to defend herself against attackers. I don't want to lose you at a young age because a wolf or a bear came at you. Or a moose with the ridiculous name of Monty!"

"I think she named him Monty, because he lives so close to five Mounties," she offered helpfully.

He was losing his patience with her. He pointed at the target. "Shoot!"

She frowned. "You don't have to yell at me!"

He took deep breaths. "Are you deliberately trying to provoke me?"

"Of course not! Why would I want someone to yell at me? I haven't lost my mind, though you may have lost yours!"

"JoAnn?"

"Yes, Kendall?"

"Would you please shoot that target so we can go home and put the gun away?"

She nodded. "I'll try. If I hit it this time, will we be done for the day?"

"Nothing would make me happier."

JoAnn took careful aim, wanting to get home before it started raining more than anything else she'd ever wanted in her life. She wanted to be done shooting more than she wanted to play music again, and that was saying something. She closed her eyes and pulled the trigger.

Kendall let out a whoop, carefully taking the gun from her hands and emptying the chamber before putting the gun into his holster. He grabbed her into a bear hug and swung her around, lifting her off her feet. "You did it! You hit the center of the target."

"I figured out the trick!" She couldn't have been happier with herself.

"What did you do this time that you didn't do the other times?"

"I closed my eyes!"

Kendall pulled away, looking down at her face. "You what?"

"I closed my eyes, and it worked!"

He sighed. "At times like this I just want to yell at you. Do you know that?"

She nodded. "You have this vein in your forehead that throbs when you get angry with me. I noticed it our first night together. Right now, it seems to be trying to play a song, because the tempo is very steady. Fast, but steady."

He shook his head at her. "Let's go home. What time is everyone going to be at our place?"

"Six. But I don't have to cook. Everyone is bringing their own dishes, and all the others are going to cook. All I have to do is play music."

"I'm sure that will thrill you. I want you to cook, and you play music. I want you to shoot, and you close your eyes. Why exactly did you come West again?"

She grinned, looping her arm through his. "Because I knew there was a very lonely Mountie who needed a bride who would keep him on his toes."

"You're doing that, all right."

"And you know why else?"

"I'm sure I couldn't begin to guess."

"Because I knew you played beautiful music, and I knew you needed me beside you, playing with you."

Kendall smiled at her. As crazy as she made him, she was right. He did need her playing with him. "I'm so glad you're here. I'm still annoyed with you for shutting your eyes when you were supposed to be shooting, but I'm glad you're here."

"Me too." It was then she realized what had happened. She'd come to the West to start a new life with a stranger, and she'd gone and fallen in love with him. That hadn't been part of the plan at all.

THE NEXT MORNING, JoAnn waited for Kendall to head to work, and then she went to see Jess.

"You need to teach me everything you know about cooking. I'll take good notes. How much can you teach me before Kendall gets home from work tonight?"

Jess stared at her friend for a moment, blinking slowly. But then a slow smile transformed her face. "You love Kendall!"

JoAnn frowned. "Is it really that obvious? Just because I want to learn to cook?"

"Just because you're in a hurry to learn so that you can make him happy. I think it's great!" Jess rubbed her hands together, excitedly. "So what do you want to learn to cook first?"

"Can we start with breakfast foods? I make the world's *best* pancakes, and I'm not quite sure how it happened, but that's the only thing I know how to make for breakfast, and I think Kendall should have options."

Jess laughed. "Sure, let's start with breakfast. Eggs?"

JoAnn shrugged, sitting down at the table and pulling out a notebook. "Let's make a list of what I want to learn first, and we'll go from there."

"Sounds good to me. You'll be the best cook in town except for me, Tilly, and anyone else who can cook!"

"Thanks for the vote of confidence."

"Anytime!"

KENDALL WAS DOING rounds with Theodore. Usually they went their separate ways, but there had been some trouble south of town, so the two of them went together rather than splitting up.

"Do you love Jess?" Kendall asked, not looking at his friend. He was embarrassed to bring up the conversation, but he needed advice, and Theodore was the only man he knew of to ask. He could write his father, but why wait?

Theodore gave Kendall a funny look. "Of course I love my wife. I wouldn't have asked her to marry me if I didn't, would I?"

"I guess not." Kendall rode on for another five minutes, trying to think of the best way to ask his next question. "How did you realize you loved her?"

"When I knew that Jess was going to leave to go back to Ottawa and everything inside me hurt at the very idea. I couldn't bear to let her go."

"Because of her cooking?"

Theodore grinned. "You know, her cooking actually had nothing to do with it. It was her. She was the sweetest, kindest, most loving woman I'd ever met. And the prettiest, of course."

"JoAnn is prettier."

"Maybe to a blind man who has nothing to do but play guitar all day."

Kendall glared at the other man. "You heard her sing. She's amazing."

"She has a voice, that's for sure. Jess can't carry a tune in a tin pail. She tried to sing in front of me once, and it was all I could do not to cover my ears and run for the hills." Theodore shrugged. "I love her anyway."

"That bad, huh? JoAnn told me that Jess wrote to her about what a wonderful singer I am, but she wasn't sure if she should believe it, because Jess is tone deaf. She said actual deaf people aren't as tone deaf as Jess is."

"Yeah, she really is that bad. But I love her, so I listened to her as if she wasn't breaking my eardrums."

Kendall laughed, shaking his head. "I don't know that I could have done that, even out of love."

"Well, when you love someone, you want them to be happy. I knew it would hurt her feelings if I ran screaming into the night, so I listened and smiled."

"I guess that's true."

Theodore looked at his friend. "Exactly where is this going, Kendall? What do you hope to achieve with this conversation?"

"I don't know. I guess I wanted to figure out whether I'm in love."

"How am I supposed to answer that? I don't live inside your head! How do you feel when you're apart from her? Can you imagine spending the rest of your life with her?"

Kendall nodded. "Sure can. I can imagine having her at my side, playing her fiddle, every day for the rest of our lives. I can imagine children and grandchildren."

"Sounds good. Now try to imagine your life without her in it."

"I'd rather not."

Theodore smiled. "I think you have your answer."

"I guess I do." What he didn't know was how he felt about it. Should he be in love with a woman who couldn't cook or clean? All she seemed to do really well is play music and sing. And kiss. Wow, the woman could kiss. And when she smiled at him, he felt like the sun had come out after a week of rain.

"Are you going to tell her when you get home?"

"Shouldn't she tell me first? What if she doesn't love me?" Kendall couldn't imagine baring his feelings like that, only to find out she didn't return his love.

"I think it's fine for you to tell her first."

"How did you know Jess loved you?"

Theodore sighed. "Well, you have to remember that I've known Jess since she was a little girl. She followed me around at recess with lovesick eyes, and one day she followed me home from school. She made up some kind of crazy excuse, but I knew then she had feelings for me. Some women are fickle and love ten men in a lifetime, but not my Jessica. I knew she was in love with me from that day on.

When Mom brought her out here to marry me, Jess thought I'd already agreed, and she was mortified."

Kendall tried to imagine JoAnn in the same situation, but he couldn't. JoAnn would have turned right around and gotten back on the train, or stolen a horse, or tried to train Mickey—err, Monty Moose to wear a saddle and carry a passenger. "That must have been really hard for her."

"I didn't handle it well either. But we spent time together during the week she was forced to stay here, and we made it work. By the time Thursday rolled around again, and the train came into town, I knew I couldn't let her go. Ever. We belong together."

"I've thought so since the moment I first saw you two together. And from the first second I tasted her bread." Kendall sighed. "Someone needs to teach JoAnn to cook the way Jess does."

Theodore looked over at Kendall for a moment. "Be careful about asking her to get better at things. I worry that it will make her feel as if she's not good enough just the way she is."

Kendall shook his head. "Not my JoAnn. She knows I think everything about her is perfect."

"I hope you're right."

AFTER HER COOKING lessons for the day, JoAnn went out to the woods and practiced target shooting. She'd never actually loaded the gun herself, but Kendall had shown her how twice, and she was sure she could handle it.

When she squeezed the trigger the first time, she remembered why she hated shooting so much. The gun kicked back at her, making her hand throb. Never mind, though. Before Kendall took her shooting again, she *would* be proficient with his handgun. She hoped to never have to shoot a living creature—but if she had to, she'd be able to, and that seemed to be the most important thing Kendall wanted from her.

As she fired over and over, she kept missing the target. As she loaded the gun for what would have to be her final time that day, she grumbled under her breath. "He hates when I shoot with my eyes closed, but that's the only thing that works for me. Let me see if it was just a fluke, or if it's a consistent thing."

She aimed, closed her eyes, and shot. Her mark was right there in the center of the target. Again and again, she shot with her eyes closed, never missing. Well apparently, that was the only way she could shoot, and Kendall would just have to be proud of her that she could do it at all.

As she thought it, she knew she'd come back and try over and over again. She wanted to make him happy, and shooting with her eyes closed didn't accomplish that.

She made sure there were no more bullets in the chamber and tucked the gun into the waistband of her skirt, wondering what her mother would think if she could see her. She cooked every day, played the fiddle, and shot a gun. Her life was so different here than it had been back in Ottawa, so much fuller and richer. She wouldn't go back to being the pampered daughter of a businessman for anything at all.

As she rushed back to the house to start supper, the sky opened up and the rain poured down onto her. She stopped where she was, shaking her fist at the sky. She would be soaked to the skin before she got home, and drying and changing her clothes would take longer than she had available to her. Supper would be late. How could she possibly be the perfect wife her husband needed her to be by fixing supper late?

When Kendall walked into the house an hour later,

JoAnn's wet hair was drawn up into a bun. He looked at her for a moment, feeling the love wash over him. She was the most important thing in his life, but he didn't know how to tell her. How had she become more important than work and music when he'd only known her ten days? There was something awfully special about her that he couldn't turn away from.

He walked to her and swept her into a kiss, pleased when she clung to his shoulders. "Supper's going to burn if you keep doing that!" she said, laughter in her eyes.

He sighed. "Sometimes supper doesn't matter as much as kissing my wife."

JoAnn laughed softly. "Tonight it matters more. Get your wet clothes off before it's time to eat."

"How long will it be?"

"I got caught in the rain too, so I got a later start than I wanted. About thirty minutes or so until it's ready."

He nodded, walking toward the bedroom. "I'll change then."

While he changed, JoAnn worked on the dinner she'd so carefully planned. Pork chops, mashed potatoes, carrots, and fresh bread. It was her first time frying pork chops, and she hoped she'd done it right. She was nervous, because she wanted everything perfect for him, but whether that would happen was up to chance. She'd done what she could.

Kendall picked up his guitar after changing, sitting down at the table to strum a song. He now knew the names of all the chords he'd been playing for years, and he couldn't wait until they had their next music lesson. Now he could not only play, but he knew what he was doing as he played as well. Who could ask for more?

JoAnn set the table while he played, trying not to be distracted by the music. What was wrong with her that she couldn't listen to music without singing, dancing, or grabbing an instrument? Other people could just enjoy it, so it had to be a problem with her.

As soon as the table was set and the food on it, she turned to him. "I made something new today, but Jess helped me, so I think it turned out all right." She was always worried when they sat down to the table. She had to be perfect so he would love her.

Kendall grinned at her, taking her hand and pulling her toward him. "I'm sure it's as wonderful as my beautiful new wife."

JoAnn smiled, but inside she felt terrible. She was anything but wonderful, and she should be. For Kendall.

9

For the next couple of weeks, JoAnn put all her efforts into cooking, cleaning, and learning to shoot. There was one event where she and Kendall had played music for the others, but that was really the only time she'd picked up either of her instruments. She even stopped singing while she was working around the house as she concentrated on her chores, knowing that they needed her full attention if she was going to be the best wife she could be.

They'd been married for about three weeks when Kendall came home at the end of a long day to find supper waiting for him on the stove, and JoAnn sitting at the table, her head resting on her arms. It took him a minute to realize she was sound asleep.

He contemplated for a minute about whether or not to wake her, but finally decided that he needed to or she'd be very uncomfortable. Her neck would be stiff if she slept that way for long. "JoAnn?"

She jumped at his voice. "I'm so sorry! I didn't mean to fall asleep. Supper's ready." She was mortified. It took so much effort to keep the house perfect at all times that she had fallen asleep waiting for him. She sprang out of the chair and hurried to the stove, stirring the chicken and dumplings.

He caught her shoulder and pulled her to him, holding her close. "You don't have to be a perfect wife, you know."

JoAnn felt tears spring to her eyes. If he was telling her she didn't have to be perfect, that meant she was still falling very short. She'd have to double her efforts. "I'm sorry it wasn't ready."

He cupped her face in his hands, kissing her softly. "Supper smells good."

She bit her lip nervously. "I hope it *is* good. I tried to make chicken and dumplings again, but this time I had Jess stand over me. Her recipe is quite a bit different from Miss Hazel's but Theodore assured me that Jess's is much better."

"I'm going to be happy either way, I'm sure." He was pleased she hadn't given up on making the dish. One of his favorite things about her was how she didn't admit defeat. She just kept trying.

"Unless I poison you!"

He chuckled. "I don't think you've ever poisoned me."

"You don't think? That means you're not sure! Did I make you sick with some of my cooking?"

"You need to stop being so nervous! Your cooking gets better every single day. I'm sure I'll be happy with how wonderful it is."

She frowned. "I hope so." She waved him toward the table. "Did it rain a lot today?"

He shook his head. "No. Not where I was, at least. Did it rain here?"

She nodded. "I had clothes on the line, and Monty Moose came and played in the clothesline again. I don't know why he likes our wet clothes so much."

She put a big bowl of the chicken and dumplings in front

of him and handed him a spoon. Watching him with her breath held as he took the first bite, she could finally breathe when he nodded at her. "Very good."

"I'm so glad!" She got herself a bowl and sat down across from him, absolutely relieved. She felt like she was finally not a failure at the wife thing if she could cook the meal that she'd messed up so badly the first time. Of course, not being a failure was far from being perfect.

While he ate, he related the story of a pig that had gotten out of one farmer's pen and run through another farmer's wheat fields. "I wasn't sure the second farmer would ever forgive him."

"What finally happened?"

"The farmer with the pig agreed to build a better pen before the end of the day, and he's going to pay restitution to the other farmer. It's not fair for the second farmer to lose money because the other man didn't build a good pen." Kendall shrugged. "It was actually pretty simple once everything was said and done, but the men couldn't come to the agreement on their own. It's a good thing there are Mounties in the area now. That could have ended in blood. Men don't allow anything to mess with their livelihood."

"Well, I'm glad you got it sorted out. Such big problems you deal with."

He shrugged. "You know, it's what a Mountie does. No problem is too big or too small. There's been a rash of stage-coach robberies as well, so I think I might have to grab one of my fellow Mounties and go and check out the area. Another coach is due that way on Monday. Maybe Theodore can go with me."

JoAnn took her first bite of the chicken and dumplings, happy that he hadn't been humoring her...they really did taste good. "Are you closer to Theodore than the others?"

He shrugged. "I'm not sure I'd say that, but I have spent

more time with him. He was the one who trained me for the territory when I arrived. I was assigned to Vancouver when I first graduated from the academy."

"Oh! I didn't realize this wasn't your first assignment."

He nodded. "I've been a Mountie for six years, but I've only been here for a few months."

"Do you have any desire to move North to work with the natives?"

He shrugged. "That was the goal of a lot of the Mounties that I trained with, but it was never really mine. I'd go if I was asked to. Really, I'd do anything I was asked, of course. It's part of the job. I really like it here, though. I like the camaraderie of the other men, and that's not something I'd get in the North."

"Because the territories are so spread out?"

"Yes. And few of the Mounties who go North take wives with them. The climate there is very harsh and difficult on women. The mosquitoes alone make most women turn tail and run."

She sighed. "If you go, I'm going with you. I might not be the bravest woman in the world, but I could do it. I promise."

He reached out and took her hand in his. "I'm not leaving you."

"Good, because I'd have to chase after you." She smiled at him, wishing she could just tell him she loved him—but she couldn't until she was the wife he needed her to be.

After supper, she washed the dishes while he played, and then she sat down for a music lesson with him, listening to him play the different chords and naming them all. He'd already mastered the treble clef, and it was time for him to move on to the bass clef.

After she'd introduced the basic notes, she hid a yawn behind her hand. "I'm so tired. Jess is going to work with me on some new meals tomorrow, so I'd better sleep."

"But...I thought we could play some music together tonight."

She shook her head. "I'd love to, but I just can't keep my eyes open." She stood up and stretched. "Are you going to come to bed right away? Or are you going to play for a while?"

He shrugged. "I'm not tired enough to sleep yet. I think I'll just play." He watched her as she went to bed, missing the wife who played music with him every night. Despite her promise that she would move North with him, he could feel her slipping away from him. They no longer did the things that had brought them together. It was as if music no longer mattered to her, and he hated that. It was their strongest bond.

JoAnn woke early the following morning, forcing her eyes to open before she was ready. She hated mornings. If she were queen of the universe, she would ban them all, and days would start at nine in the morning instead of five.

She quickly washed her face and dressed, going into the kitchen to make a special breakfast for Kendall. Jess had taught her to make omelets the previous day, and she wanted to show off her new skill. She had saved some leftover ham in the icebox, and she was happy to be able to use it in his eggs.

When Kendall woke, he walked into the kitchen, smiling when he realized she wasn't making pancakes. Lately the pancakes had been interspersed with different breakfast foods, and though he missed the culinary delight, he'd enjoyed the variety. Of course, he'd have eaten pancakes every day of his life if that was what she'd needed him to do. "What are you making this morning?"

"Ham and cheese omelets. I thought they'd be a nice change. The coffee's ready. Sit down and I'll pour you a cup." JoAnn was unsure why the man, capable Mountie that he was, couldn't pour his own cup of coffee in the mornings, but she'd been assured that it was her job to pour it for him. So she did. She'd do anything it took to make him happy.

Kendall gladly accepted the coffee and smiled at the omelet. "You should make pancakes tomorrow morning," he said.

Jess frowned. She'd worked so hard to learn to make new things, and he only wanted her to cook the things she'd been able to cook when she arrived. She wasn't sure what she was doing wrong, but she'd work harder. Surely soon he'd see that she was the perfect wife for him.

Kendall rode out with Theodore on Monday morning, trying to surprise the stage coach robbers. They always seemed to hide in the same place. "I think JoAnn wants to go back to Ottawa," he said, as they rode off to the ambush spot, hoping to find the men who were causing so many problems.

"What makes you say that? Jess told me she's doing everything she can to be a good wife to you."

Kendall rubbed the back of his neck. "That's just the thing. She was a great wife when she got here. She played music with me, and we enjoyed each other's company. Now all she does is work. Dinner's on the table when I get home. My clothes are always in perfect order. Do you know when we went shooting yesterday, she hit the target ten times out of ten? Of course, she still won't open her eyes when she shoots, but if she's hitting the target every time, I can't complain about that, right?"

"Why do you want her to shoot?"

"I think she should be able to defend herself. Especially with Monty Moose wandering around."

Theodore shook his head. "That stupid moose. I wish Jess would let me shoot him so she could make me a delicious moose stew...but she said he's a pet and we can't shoot him. Why can't she be like a normal woman and get a puppy?"

Kendall shrugged. "No idea. I can say the same for JoAnn, though. All the ladies think that stupid moose is a pet. Don't they realize he can't sit on their laps?"

"I guess not. The female mind will always be a mystery to me. I swear I think they lie awake at night trying to think up ways to confound us."

"Not JoAnn. She works so hard, she's asleep before her head hits the pillow. I caught her sleeping at the table when I got home from work one day last week. I think I need to stop being a Mountie and move back East with her so she can live the life she's used to." Kendall was at a loss for what else to do. He couldn't let JoAnn work herself into an early grave.

"Have you asked her if that's what she wants?" Theodore asked, frowning. "I get the impression from Jess that she's happy here."

"How could she be? She's working nonstop. Her hands were soft when she arrived, and now they have calluses. Well, she always had calluses on her fingertips from playing her instruments, but those are going away, and she has calluses on her palms from hard work. She shouldn't have those!"

"Calm down, Kendall. You're going to have to sit down and talk to your wife. Don't jump to conclusions."

"I'm not jumping to conclusions. I've analyzed the situation, and there's no doubt in my mind what's best for her." Kendall shook his head. "I need to make sure she's happy. She can't be happy when she's working herself to death."

"She's nowhere close to death. She's just *tired*. We think we're doing the hard thing by being out all day working, but

I'd rather do what we do than spend all day cooking, cleaning, and doing whatever else the women do all day every day."

"What *do* they do?" Kendall asked, confused.

"Well, from what I understand, *your* wife is spending all
her time trying to learn to cook and shoot to please you."

"Why doesn't she know she already pleases me?"

"Have you told her?" Theodore asked. "Because I'm sure
that would help."

Kendall shook his head. "No, telling her will never work. I
have to find a way to show her."

"Kendall, you are never going to succeed at marriage until
you learn to communicate with your wife. Have you told her
you love her yet? That would go a long way toward making
her happy, I guarantee."

"Well, no. I'm waiting for her to tell me. I don't want to
feel stupid if I say it and she just sits there staring at me."

Theodore sighed. "We're almost there, so we can't
continue this, but you have got to learn to talk to your wife."

JOANN COULDN'T STOP FALLING asleep. Jess was teaching her
to make a chicken pot pie for supper, and she couldn't stay
awake long enough to pay attention to the lesson. Jess shook
her shoulder. "I think you need to go home and take a nap."

"Nap? No way. I'll never get everything done if I start
taking naps. You don't take naps."

"No, I really don't, but I would if I needed to. You need to.
You're spending all your time doing stuff you hate. I think
tonight you need to come to supper at my house, and you
and Kendall should play music for the rest of us."

"I can't start accepting supper invitations until I'm ready
to reciprocate."

"You *are* ready to reciprocate...besides, have you never heard of singing for your supper? Your skills lie in pleasing everyone else. You don't need to be like the rest of us."

JoAnn shook her head. "I have to learn to cook. Kendall will never love me if I don't become a good wife."

"Oh, sweetie...I think Kendall already loves you. Have you talked to him about it?"

"Well, no. But how can I? If I tell him I love him, and he doesn't respond, I'll be humiliated!"

Jess sat down at the table with her friend, ignoring the half-made chicken pot pie. "Someone has to say the words first. What if he's spending all his time worrying that you don't love him?"

"No way. Kendall doesn't worry about anything."

"Go home. Take a nap. You guys are coming over for supper tonight. You're too exhausted to cook, and that's that. I'll invite the others, and you two can play and sing, and we'll all dance. A good time will be had by all." When JoAnn started to respond, Jess shook her head. "A good time that the rest of us can't have without your music. We can all cook. We can't all play and sing."

JoAnn got to her feet, a bit unsteady with exhaustion. "I guess I'll bake a cake then."

"No! If you show up with food, I promise you I'll accidentally drop it. You will *nap* today. Be well rested so you and Kendall can play music tonight. That's all we want or need you to do."

JoAnn nodded tiredly. "Fine. I'll go sleep. But I refuse to like it."

Jess laughed. "Go away!"

JoAnn went home and crawled straight into bed, not even removing her apron. Jess was right. She needed a night to only sing for her supper. She'd go back to being the kind of wife Kendall needed tomorrow. For tonight, she'd be the musician she'd been born to become.

———

KENDALL WALKED into the cabin at the end of the day, feeling an eerie stillness. He and Theodore had managed to catch their criminals, and they were sitting in the jail there in the Mountie office. It had been a job well done, and the two of them were mighty proud of the work they'd done.

Searching the house, he finally found JoAnn sound asleep in bed. He sat down beside her, shaking her shoulder gently. "Hey. Are you all right?"

JoAnn sat up, blinking slowly. "I slept longer than I'd planned. I'm so sorry!"

Kendall shook his head. "You're allowed to sleep when you're tired."

She leaned forward, resting her head on his shoulder. "We're going to Theodore and Jess's house for supper tonight. Jess said we'd provide the music, and the other ladies would provide the food. She thought I needed a night away from cooking."

"I agree with her. You're too fragile for all the work you've been doing. I think this life is much too hard for you. Have you considered going back to Ottawa?"

JoAnn felt her stomach sink. He didn't want her. She was such a bad wife he was sending her back home to her parents. How would she ever hold her head up again? "I'll work harder."

"I don't want you to work harder! You're working too hard already!" He shook his head. "We'll have this discussion later. For now, we need to get our instruments and go play and sing for our friends. If we're singing for our supper, we need to be there on time and do a good job of it."

JoAnn nodded, not letting her tears show. She wouldn't let him see how much he'd hurt her. Later, when the lights were out, she could cry herself to sleep. For now, she'd go play music like it was the last time she was ever going to play for her friends...and it very well could be. She wondered if he was going to make her leave on the train on Thursday, or if he'd let her stay a little longer than that. Either way, she was leaving her friends, her husband, and the moose she'd grown to love.

10

*T*he whole while they played and sang that night, JoAnn smiled, doing everything she could to hold the tears at bay. Knowing Kendall wanted to end their marriage and send her back to Ottawa made her feel like she'd truly failed at something for the first time in her entire life.

They played before and after supper, watching as the happy couples whirled around them. Why did all of the others seem so happy, when she was fighting for her marriage with everything she had left? What was wrong with her that she couldn't make her man happy when all the other women could?

As they walked the short distance to their cabin, their instruments in their cases to protect them from the ever-constant rain, JoAnn fought against her emotions. She didn't want to stay where she wasn't wanted, but she so badly wanted to stay.

When they walked into the cabin, she set her violin down before turning to him. "You can't send me away. I've worked too hard to learn to be the kind of wife you need! I can do better!"

Kendall gaped at her in shock. "I'm *not* sending you away! I'm going to stop being a Mountie and move back to the city with you. I just can't watch you slowly kill yourself working so hard!" How could she even think he'd send her away? Had she lost her mind?

"But you *love* being a Mountie. And I'm not killing myself. I'm just learning to work hard. Every other woman in the West does it, and I can do it too."

He stepped closer to her, ready to shake some sense into her. "I do love being a Mountie, but I love being your husband more." He stared at her for a moment. "I love *you* more!"

"I refuse to let you give up your position as a Mountie to move to the city, when I know you'd hate it! I—wait, what did you say?"

"I love being your husband more than I love being a Mountie!"

"No, after that."

He smiled, gathering her close to him. "I love *you* more than being a Mountie. I love you more than I ever dreamed I could love someone." He brushed his lips across her forehead. "Is that what you meant?"

"That's exactly what I meant! I love you too, you big idiot!"

"Idiot? Did you just call me an idiot?" He shook his head at her. "You can't call me an idiot and tell me you love me all in one sentence!"

"Well, I just did. I've been working from dawn to dusk to be the best wife I could be so you'd love me."

"Who's the idiot now? I've been in love with you for *weeks!*"

"You have?" She shook her head. "But I couldn't cook or clean or do any of those wifely things!"

He sighed. "I didn't need you to be able to do those things to love you. I needed you to be you. To play music with me. To play chess with me. Do you know tonight's the first time we've played music together in weeks?"

"I've been too tired, because it takes too much energy to cook and clean and sew buttons and darn socks. Do you know how much I hate your *darn socks*?"

"I wanted you to be able to cook something I could eat, but you could have made pancakes every day for months, and I'd have been happy. I didn't need you to learn to make all kinds of fancy eggs and stuff. I just needed to have edible food."

She searched his face. "You don't need me to be the perfect wife?"

"Why would I need that? I fell in love with the girl who messed up the chicken and dumplings and played music with me. Do you know how much more confident I feel about my guitar playing now that I can read music? You've changed my life in so many ways."

She buried her face against his chest and let the tears fall. "I worked so hard to be good enough, and I was good enough to start?" She sniffled loudly. "I feel like an utter nincompoop."

He held her tightly. "Don't cry. Now I feel like I've hurt you. I wanted to move back to Ottawa because I thought the hard work of living in the West and being a Mountie's wife was making you too sad to play your music. If you stopped playing, the world would be a terrible place."

She looked up at him, the tears still clinging to her lashes. "I stopped playing because I was too tired trying to be what I thought you wanted me to be. Now that I know you don't care, I'll just make easy meals and play my music more."

"I like that idea. And when people want you to come over and sing so they can dance, you need to *let* them feed us. We're working hard to make their lives better, so they can pay us in food. Doesn't bother me a bit."

She laughed. "So if I want a quilt made, I should sing for the others while they make it instead of helping them?"

"Sure! If you can talk them into working while you play, who am I to argue with that?"

"You know what, Kendall?"

He shook his head. "No, what?"

"I like the way you think. Well, I like the way you're thinking right now, but not the way you think when you want me to go back to Ottawa."

He frowned. "I still think we should go back East. I think life here is too hard for you. I can't ask you to give up the lifestyle you were born to so you can cook and clean for me. It wouldn't be right."

"I tell you what. I will stop trying to be the perfect Western wife if you will stop threatening to take me back East."

He took her hand and pulled her over to the table, sitting down and pulling her into his lap. "I can't let you keep working so hard."

She sighed. "But that's what I'm saying. I'll stop working so hard. I don't want you to give up everything you've spent your whole life working for. I mean, they'd take away your red serge jacket!"

He laughed. "You only love me for my red serge!"

"Nah...I love the hat too. The *whole uniform*."

He pulled her down and kissed her. "Let's make a deal."

She eyed him skeptically. "What kind of deal?"

"I was thinking that we'd try this for a year. If at the end of the year, you're unhappy, then we'll move to Ottawa, and

I'll find a job there. I could still be a policeman, but maybe not a Mountie anymore."

"Why would you be a policeman if you couldn't wear red serge?"

"Are you going to be serious at all?"

She sighed. "Yes, I can agree with that deal…but I won't be unhappy, because I'll be married to the man I love."

He shrugged. "I hope that's the case. But if it's not, I promise you, we'll go East. I can't risk you being unhappy."

"I'm sure a lot of wives are unhappy, Kendall. It's just how life works."

"Not my life, and not my wife."

She snugged closer to him. "I love it when you rhyme."

"It's a deal, though, right?"

JoAnn nodded. "Sure. I won't be unhappy, so it really doesn't matter now, does it?"

SEPTEMBER 1911

"ARE you sure you don't want to go back East? You should be with your mother!" Kendall looked at her worriedly.

"I don't *want* to be with my mother. Women have babies every day. What's different about me?" JoAnn thought he was being ridiculous. She patted her round belly affectionately.

He shrugged. "You've always been pampered. You shouldn't be having babies in the middle of nowhere. You should have a doctor attending you."

"Jess did fine without a doctor. So will I."

"Jess is made of hardier stock than you. She was raised without all the wealth and privilege you had." Kendall knew he was making no sense, but he wanted her to have proper medical facilities for having the baby.

JoAnn glared at him. "You've spent the last year holding my background against me. You've just been waiting for a reason to send me back to Ottawa. Well let me tell *you* something, Constable Jameson. I'm happy here. I'm happy being married to you, and I'm happy living in British Columbia. I'm even happy having a moose for a pet! So you are not sending me back home, because I refuse to go! I'm having this baby right here! Today!"

"What do you mean today? You said the baby was due at the beginning of October. The baby can't come yet. We're not ready!"

"*You* may not be ready, but I am. I've been making clothes for the baby, and they're all ready. There are blankets and sleepers. I even learned to knit so I could make the baby little tiny booties." She shrugged. "Whether you're ready or not, this baby is coming."

"But…I haven't given you the gift I made for the baby, and your mother isn't here!"

"My mother doesn't *need* to be here. You need to stop panicking. Get me the gift for the baby, and go get Jess. She'll help me with the labor." Her mother? What did her mother have to do with anything?

His eyes widened. "Jess hasn't been trained in first aid. How is she supposed to help with the baby! I'm the one with training!"

"You may have training, but you're also the one panicking. Go get Jess, and get me the gift. I can look at it while I labor."

"I can't leave you while you're having the baby!"

She sighed. "First babies take a long time to arrive. I've been reading about this for months, and I helped Jess with her baby, remember?"

"I remember, but I can't leave you!"

"Kendall, if you don't leave me, I'm going to take your guitar and bash you over the head with it, because you're making me absolutely crazy. Go. Get. Jess."

He left the cabin, still grumbling. She should have better conditions to give birth in. Her mother should be there. He ran next door to get Jess. "JoAnn's in labor. She wants you! Hurry!"

Jess grinned at the panicked look in Kendall's eyes. She looked over her shoulder at Theodore. "Good thing it's a Sunday and everyone's home. I just fed Jack, and he's content for a while. Bring him to me if he gets hungry. I'm going to go deliver Jack's best friend...or future bride. I'd be content with either!"

Theodore looked up from the book he was reading. "All right. Happy birthing!"

Jess laughed and waved as she walked next door. She wasn't sure why, but Kendall had run toward Joel's cabin. She ignored the man and checked on her friend. "How are you feeling?" she asked as she opened the door.

"Kendall's making me crazy, but other than that, I think I'm all right. I've been walking, because that seems to help the pains."

"You're a little early, but not too much. Do you know how far apart the pains are?"

"A couple of minutes. I've got some time. Kendall's supposed to be fetching the gift he made me, but I will never forgive you if you let him back in this house. The man has been trying to send me back East all morning, and I'm not going!"

"He thinks your mother should be here," Jess said with a grin. "I can't imagine your mother helping in a situation like this. She'd just get in the way."

JoAnn grinned. "I don't think you're giving her enough credit. She did give birth a few times."

"I know...but I can't see her being good while someone else is in labor. She's more the type to call in the midwife and serve tea."

JoAnn laughed. "I'm glad you're here with me. I can't imagine going through such an important moment without you beside me."

"I wish Lisa was here. But I'm glad she's happy now, too."

"If only she could be happy *here*!" JoAnn said, stopping to lean against the wall as she had another pain.

Kendall carried in a cradle then. He set it on the floor next to where JoAnn was leaning. "What can I do to help?"

"Would you go spend the day with Theodore? Please? I want to have this baby without worrying about you getting upset with every pain." JoAnn loved Kendall more than she could express, but she needed to be able to concentrate on having the baby.

Kendall walked to her and kissed her softly. "I'll be right next door if you need me. Remember we're all trained in first aid if anything goes—"

"Nothing's going to go wrong," Jess told him. "Go on and spend the day with Theodore and Jack. Have fun. Don't come back until I tell you."

"What about food?"

Jess frowned. "Good point. Tell Tilly we'll need some soup in a couple of hours. I don't want JoAnn having anything solid until after the baby's born."

Kendall nodded, pleased to have a job other than sitting with Theodore. "I want to know as soon as the baby is born!"

"You'll be the first to know," Jess promised. "Now, go! She'll be able to labor easier without you here."

Kendall nodded, hurrying to leave. He didn't want to go,

but if it made JoAnn more comfortable, then he wasn't going to stay.

JoAnn shook her head. "Now I miss him." She knew she was being irrational, and that was one of the reasons she wanted him to leave, but she wanted him back.

Jess just shook her head. "I was the same way when I was in labor. Just push through it. We'll handle it together."

"You'll stay with me?"

"Of course I will!"

———

It was almost twelve hours later when Jess went to get Kendall. Tilly had kindly provided meals for Jess and JoAnn, and ended up staying. Jess hurried into her cabin and found Theodore asleep and Kendall pacing the floor. "It's over. JoAnn's asking for you."

"She's okay?" Kendall looked scared.

"She's doing great, and so is the baby. Come see!"

Kendall got up and rushed to his home, throwing the door wide. He found JoAnn sitting up in bed, cradling the baby in her arms. He forgot about everything and everyone else, sitting on the edge of the bed. "How are you feeling?"

JoAnn gave him a huge smile. "I'm fine. We have a future wife for little Jack. What should we name her?"

He stared down at the baby in her arms. "A girl? We really had a girl?"

She nodded. "You're not disappointed?"

"How could I be? I hope she grows up to play the fiddle just like her mama."

JoAnn laughed. "And the guitar! Don't forget the guitar!"

"Should we name her Hazel? Since Miss Hazel is the one who brought us together?" he asked, wondering if he could hold the baby, but not wanting to take her from JoAnn yet.

"I like that. Hazel it is." She looked at the baby, asking, "What do you think of the name Hazel?"

"You don't expect her to really answer you, do you?"

She laughed softly. "I'm not that crazy. She's sleeping. I'll ask her again when she wakes up." Her eyes met Kendall's. "I just made it through labor without being back East and without my mother. I hope this effectively proves once and for all that I don't need to go back to Ottawa. I'm perfectly content here with you and little Hazel. I wonder how Miss Hazel will react to having a namesake."

"I'm sure she'll love it! Especially if we tell her that we've already arranged the marriage between her and little Jack." He reached out and touched the baby's cheek with the back of his finger. "I can't believe she's ours."

JoAnn smiled. "You'll believe it in the middle of the night when she's waking up to eat."

"Have I told you yet today that I love you? And I'm so glad you're the bride that stepped off that train to marry me. I wouldn't trade you for the best cook in all of British Columbia!"

"Good, because we know the two best, and I wouldn't want to have to be jealous of them!" She smiled at him, her blue eyes twinkling. "I love you, Kendall Jameson. I'm so glad you're in my life."

"I love you, too!"

AN EXCERPT FROM A BRIDE FOR ELIJAH

"*G*et your hands off me, you filthy swine." Rose pulled her hand back and was already bringing the palm of it across his cheek as the door opened. The loud gasp that reached her ears drowned out the crack of her hand on the man's skin. Slowly turning her head, she knew the moment she saw her mother and the other woman standing there, they weren't going to believe anything she had to say.

They'd already made up their minds.

She was in the arms of Robert Harvey, with the front of her dress torn just enough to expose the white of her skin underneath. It wouldn't matter if she tried to say she'd been fighting him off, because everyone knew Robert was the man who'd been chosen for her to marry. He was one of the most sought-after bachelors in all of Ottawa. And the man who'd been chosen to partner in her father's law firm.

All this meant was that there would be no way she could get out of marrying him.

While some things had come a long way in the past few decades, a woman's reputation could still be destroyed in one instance. She could then be forced to marry the man who she'd been caught alone with in the society she lived in—the wealthy elite of Ottawa.

Well, she wasn't going to end up stuck being married to a man she despised, no matter what damage her reputation suffered.

"Mother. Mrs. Franks." Nodding to the women, she tried to walk by them with her head held high, while pulling her blouse back over to cover herself. As she got beside them, her skirt got caught on a metal vase sitting near the doorway, and the entire pot overturned with a loud crash.

She stopped and tightly clenched her eyes briefly, not even wanting to turn around to see the damage she'd just done. Of course she wouldn't be able to make an exit with her dignity intact.

Taking a deep breath, she continued walking, never looking back. She'd rather be sent through the gates of hell, forced to sit with the devil himself, than to end up married to Robert Harvey. So, with the sound of the vase still rolling and echoing loudly across the room, she made her feet take one step in front of the other as she kept going out the door.

No, this time, she was going to take matters into her own hands. She wasn't sure how yet, but she knew she was going to have to leave the sheltered existence she'd lived in Ottawa behind.

And she realized with a start, she'd never been more excited in her life.

SHE HATED LYING, but she didn't see any other way around it. Her plan was already in motion, and by the time anyone realized what she'd done, it would be too late to do anything about it.

"I'm sure going to miss you, Rose."

Rose set her bag down and went over to put her arms around her friend. Claire Anderson was a maid who worked at their house, but Rose had never thought of her as anything less than a friend. She'd been her confidante, and often the only one to show her any compassion or kindness while Rose's parents worked so hard to rise in the ranks of Ottawa society.

The girls often snuck away together to talk to each other about their dreams and what they hoped for their future. Claire was a hopeless romantic, and she believed in true love. Rose wanted to believe in that too, but from what she'd seen in her own parent's marriage, she wasn't sure it was real.

"I know, Claire. I wish you could come with me. I promise to write, and maybe someday, you can come out there to see me." Rose tried to keep her lip from trembling as she pulled back and looked into her friend's tear-filled eyes.

She knew it was unlikely that Claire could ever afford to travel out west. And Rose doubted she'd ever be welcomed back here in Ottawa once her parents found out what she'd done. So truthfully, they both knew it was probably the last time they would see each other.

"What is he like? Did Miss Hazel tell you much about him? Is he handsome?"

Rose smiled as Claire asked the very questions she'd known her friend would ask. It was the first time they'd really had a chance to sit and talk alone since Miss Hazel Hughes had approached Rose at church on Sunday. She would be heading to begin her training in just a few days, so she had been secretly trying to pack more of her belongings than anyone knew.

Her parents believed she was being trained in the wifely duties for her marriage to Robert. They couldn't understand why she was insisting on the training since Robert would be a partner in her father's law firm, and they would have maids as she was accustomed to.

Rose had insisted she wanted to be the best wife possible. She wanted to go to Miss Hazel's to learn everything she could before getting married.

Claire was the only one who knew the truth.

She had no intentions of marrying Robert, and would be leaving on a train heading to British Columbia on the first of October. And when she arrived, Rose would be marrying a stranger.

A Mountie who Miss Hazel Hughes had met, and who she'd decided needed a wife.

"I don't know any more than I've already told you. Miss Hazel says that Elijah is a kind and quiet man, and he needs someone who can bring out the laughter in him. And most importantly, he will protect me if I need it."

Claire wrinkled her eyes together like she always did when she was annoyed. "Robert Harvey better not even think of chasing you out there. If he does, I hope your Mountie takes care of him and lets him know that you're no longer someone he can try bending to his will."

Rose rolled her eyes. "He's not my Mountie, Claire." Although she had to admit to feeling a certain tingle in her stomach as she said the words. She knew it was crazy to be running across the country to marry a stranger, but somehow she sensed that this man Elijah would treat her better than the man she'd be forced to marry if she stayed here.

This way, she could have some control of her own life, and get away from the stifling life she led under her parent's watchful eyes.

"I still can't believe Hazel Hughes just came right up to you and said she thought you'd be perfect as a Mountie's wife where her son was working. Or that you'd be so quick to agree for that matter!"

"Trust me, when Miss Hazel has an idea, she doesn't back down easily. I knew the minute she came over to me she had something in mind. I've spoken to her quite a few times over the years at church, so I could tell she wasn't just coming to make small talk."

Rose was leaning into her wardrobe, carefully choosing which dresses she would take with her as she talked with Claire. She hadn't realized quite how far she had her head inside until a loud clap startled her, making her bang her head on the corner of a small wardrobe shelf.

As Claire's voice followed, saying how romantic it all sounded, Rose had difficulty hearing through the ringing in her ears. She reached up to rub the spot that had been wounded as she quickly spun around to glare at her friend.

"Claire, look what you made me do! I just hit my head so hard I'm seeing stars. Get the notion out of your own head that this is some kind of romantic trip I'm going on."

Claire just laughed. "Rose, you and I both know you'd have likely banged your head regardless of what I was doing." She clapped her hands again for emphasis. "And, I have a feeling you might be in for more than you even realize when you head out to marry your Mountie."

Rose just kept massaging the bump that was already forming and shook her head in Claire's direction.

"I've told you already, he's not my Mountie!"

ABOUT THE AUTHOR

www.kirstenandmorganna.com

Printed in Great Britain
by Amazon